DEADLINE

Deadline

Scarlet Hawthorne

Charlotte's Letters Publishing

2014 Charlotte's Letters Publishing Edition
www.CharlottesLetters.com

Charlotte's Letters Publishing: An imprint of Southern Girl Press
2707 8th Avenue, New York, New York 10030

ISBN-13: 978-0692321683
ISBN-10: 0692321683

DEDICATION

To M

ACKNOWLEDGMENTS

I am most grateful to Chuck Hustmyre for suggesting I write a story about "a raunchy sex author who goes out to some secluded cabin in the woods and is stalked and attacked," as well as for providing the title. I would also like to thank him for his assistance with my research on criminal investigations.

I must express my appreciation to DP Lyle, MD, for his invaluable information and insight in forensic science and for not wincing at my more unsavory scenarios.

Thanks also to my beta readers for their encouragement and enthusiasm, and to the one anonymous employee of the New York City Police Department who did not transfer me for the eighteenth time and actually answered my questions.

Finally, a special thank you to my husband for his loving support and constant willingness to take a "hands-on" approach for the additional research required to write this novel.

And of Jezebel also spake the LORD, saying, The dogs shall eat Jezebel. I Kings 21:23

When Jezebel heard about it, she put on eye makeup, arranged her hair and looked out of a window. II Kings 9:30

And they went to bury her: but they found no more of her than the skull, and the feet, and the palms of her hands. II Kings 9:35

Chapter 1

Sarah arrived at the twelfth-floor penthouse in the Flatiron District via the keycard elevator and walked across the marble floor of the foyer. "Knock-knock!"

"In the kitchen," Gillian called out.

Sarah followed her voice across the white oak hardwood flooring through the open spacious living area, furnished throughout in rich, creamy tones with black accents. The windows along the kitchen and dining area caught her attention before she even glanced at her client.

"Wow. I will never get used to that view."

Gillian stood with a mug in her hand on the other side of the extensive marble-topped island wearing a long-sleeved black jacket dress and black boots, the shoulder-length red hair fringing her forehead accentuating her dark eye make-up. "And that's the north side. Do you want some coffee?"

"No, thanks."

"You and Jacob should move in. This place was way too big for two people, and now it's just me. Kind of ironic. When we started looking for places in the City, Martin chose this one because of the view, and he didn't even stick around to enjoy it."

Sarah turned to her friend. "So have you heard from him?"

"Nope, and I don't expect to. He's moved on to younger and thinner pastures. Last thing before leaving for London, I signed the final divorce papers." She rinsed out her coffee cup and put it into the empty dishwasher. "Sure you don't want to join me in the *ivory tower*? I won't even charge you rent."

"You know Jacob will never leave Brooklyn," Sarah said, shaking her head and rolling her eyes. "Believe me, I've tried. He doesn't think the City is a good place to raise kids."

"What, it's not Mars. Wait a sec…Holy crap! Are you pregnant?"

"No, but he really wants to give it a go again. Over forty, you know. Cue the *Jaws* theme music. *Duh-dun…Duh-dun…*"

"You know, the reference to the *Jaws* theme song is kind of a giveaway."

"Of course, we haven't exactly been *trying*, if, *ahem*, you know what I mean."

"You two aren't having any problems, are you?"

"Uh, no. Not really. Just both busy. Barely see each other, and when we do, we're too tired."

"Well, don't neglect your husband on my account. I'd hate for our success to cost us *both* a failed marriage."

"No worries there."

"I love your hair. Did you change it?"

Sarah swept her hand down the long blond locks. "I went lighter. You think it looks OK?"

"Yeah, I think it's great! You look quite…posh."

Sarah laughed. "*Posh*, huh? London rubbing off on you? Jacob hates it, but I like it. So how are you feeling?"

"Exhausted. Even in first class, I didn't get much sleep on the plane. I'm such a parvenu, I didn't want to miss any of the courses—of course, when have I ever. Plus I kept drinking wine and watching movies."

"Yeah, rub it in."

"Hey, I tried to get you to come with me. And, besides, you can afford first class on your own now."

"I know, but I had to stay here and keep your book launch on schedule. Plus Jacob couldn't get away, and I didn't want to go without him."

"Ah, yes, the smug-marrieds, and now I'm twice divorced."

"Maybe I'm a bad luck charm. Next time you get married, you might want to consider getting someone else to be your maid of honor."

"I don't see myself getting married again. Most men will either be intimidated by my success like Martin or only be after me for my money."

"That might not be so bad. You could get yourself a little boy toy. Maybe one of those cover models."

"Ha, ha. You know they are only interested in anorexics or other cover models. Regardless, that's not my type."

"I didn't think Martin was either."

"I guess he agrees with you." She covered her yawn with her hand. "Listen, next time, please don't schedule a book signing the day after I come back from across some ocean. I think I'm still on London time, and I haven't had hardly any sleep."

"Sorry, but that was the publisher's publicity department—not me!"

"All I've done for weeks is publicity. At least in London they don't think I'm a fat cow because I'm not a size six."

"Just stop! You're gorgeous and you know it."

"Tell that to the tabloids. If I hear the word *zaftig* one more time, I'm going to puke."

"Stop reading tabloids. Problem solved. Besides, this is the kind of signing you like, an independent neighborhood bookstore. Are you about ready to go? We have the car with the banners and everything."

"It's still not going to be easy to maintain a smile when I feel like shit. Where is Jacob, anyway?"

"There was no place to park, so he's driving around the block until we go down." She crossed the living area toward the floor-to-ceiling windows leading to the south-side terrace. "I wonder if I can see him from here."

Gillian used a remote control to open the folding glass doors, and immediately the sounds from the city street below poured in. She followed Sarah, who walked out onto the terrace, staring out at the skyline. "Damn, I wish we could leave Brooklyn."

"Well, the City isn't always what it's cracked up to be."

As if on cue, an ear-splitting, high-pitched squeal from above caused them both to cringe. "What the hell is that?"

"*Ugh!* That is my upstairs neighbor's hot tub. There's something wrong with the fucking thing.

That's why I couldn't get any sleep when I got home! First that whining wove its way into my dreams, and I ended up in a dentist's office having a tooth drilled. Then the throbbing in my skull awoke me to *this* nightmare. I thought they would have had it fixed by now. Come on. I can't take it. Let's go downstairs and find your husband."

They took the elevator down to the lobby, and as they walked out, Gillian spoke to the doorman. "Chris!"

"Yes, Mrs. Tate?"

"That hot tub over my bedroom is still not fixed!"

"I'm sorry, Mrs. Tate. I'll speak with maintenance about it."

"And how often does one man have to sit in a hot tub, anyway? Am I going to have to buy the rooftop penthouse just so I don't have to live with that squeal?"

As he held the door open for the two women to exit, he said, "Mrs. Tate, I promise, I will speak to maintenance first thing Monday morning."

Gillian turned back to him. "Chris, it isn't 'Mrs.' Tate any more. I guess just 'Ms.' will do."

Jacob sat in the sedan parked just outside the stone and iron building waiting for them with the engine on. "Hi, Gillian," he said as she slid in the backseat while Sarah sat up front.

"Hi, Jacob. I hope you haven't been sitting out here long. You should have come up."

"No, I know if I do that, I'll have to hear it from this one," he said, hooking a thumb toward his wife, "how we should move to Manhattan."

"Because it would be more convenient for my work," Sarah said.

"Not for mine."

"C'mon. You can practice law anywhere. All the publishing houses and other agents are in Manhattan."

Gillian leaned her head back against the seat and closed her eyes. She had drifted off when she heard Jacob say her name. "Did you tell Gillian yet?"

She sat up with a frown. "Tell Gillian what?"

Sarah blew out an aggravated breath. "Well, I have good news and bad news."

"Good news first."

"*Pricked with Thorns* released on top of the bestseller lists for both the *Times* and *USA Today*."

"You're kidding? Wow, Jack really did know what he was talking about with MMF. So what's the bad news?"

"Your publisher has been receiving letters," Jacob answered.

"Letters?"

"Just like the emails and comments on your blog," Sarah said. "This group called the Sword of Michael the Archangel sent a couple of harassing letters along the lines of their blog comments."

Gillian stared out the window as they sputtered along through New York City traffic. "What else is new? Even before the second novel hit bookstores, they've been spewing out all those anti-gay Bible verses. None of the hate comments have been posted on the blog, have they?"

"No, they're moderated and have to be approved, but the publicity staffer managing your blog still sees them." Sarah twisted her neck to look at Gillian behind her. "Some of these more recent messages were kind of different. I think they were more aimed at your divorce."

"How so?"

"They were all about how a wife should submit to her husband."

"Yeah, I wish," Gillian said under her breath, then she sat up, facing forward. "How would they even know about my divorce?"

"I...I'm sorry, Gillian. Somehow the press got a hold of it."

She closed her eyes and let her head fall back. "Great. Has Martin spoken to any reporters?"

"No, not that I know of. But what about this group? Are you ready to go to the police yet?"

"Of course not. Over a few letters and emails? I'm not going to let these crackpots intimidate me."

"Gillian," Jacob said, "I'm not telling you to go to the police or anything, but I do think you should take these threats seriously."

"I have too many other things to think about besides these homophobic, misogynistic nutjobs. I have to get this damn third novel finished."

Jacob rattled out a lengthy breath, heavy with aggravation. "So what's this one going to be about? Is this another male/male thing?"

Before she could answer, Gillian's cell phone vibrated in her pocket. "Speak of the devil," she said, glancing at the picture on the screen before answering. "Hi, Jack. What's up?"

"You bitch! You're back and you didn't even call?"

With a soft laugh, she pressed her finger and thumb against her eyes without rubbing the makeup. "I'm sorry. I am so exhausted, you have no idea. And I'm on my way to a book signing right now."

"So I guess that means you don't want to go out clubbing with me later."

She yawned. "Thanks, but I have to get some rest and get back to writing the final novel in the ménage trilogy. I'm working on a deadline here, and it's getting closer while I'm not getting any further along."

"You're sure you don't need to do any more research?"

With humor in her tone, she said, "I think I've spent enough time in gay dance clubs for *several* trilogies! I just need some peace and quiet. I thought I might be able to get some writing done in London, but it was just one promotional appearance after another. Now I get back and find out that, on top of more harassing letters from that Michael the Archangel group, the end of my marriage has become public knowledge. I love that my husband dumping me has become fodder for the tabloids."

"Yeah, I'm sorry, hon. The offer to use my parents' cabin in the Adirondacks still stands. It's the off-season, so you'll have plenty of peace and quiet."

"Thanks, Jack, but I just need to lock myself in my apartment and get cranking away on this story. I haven't even finished the outline yet." They pulled up outside the bookstore, where already a long line of readers were lined up outside for a chance to meet *P.G. Tate.* "Jesus." She leaned her head back again, shielding her eyes with her hand. "We just got to the signing. I hope I don't fall asleep mid-signature."

"Aw, my poor darling. Well, give me a call tomorrow after you've had some rest."

After more than three hours, Sarah checked on her client. "We're done. You OK?"

Sitting in front of banners emblazoned with the covers of her first two successful novels, Gillian dropped her head down onto her hands on the tabletop. "When they talk about writer's cramp, I never thought it would be from inscribing books."

Sarah rubbed her hand between Gillian's shoulder blades. "Poor baby. What a problem to have!"

"I hate being the object of pity, all the 'sympathetic' comments about my marriage, and my cheeks ache from smiling so much."

"You ready to go? Jacob's pulling the car around. You want me to go ahead and take the banners down?"

Gillian sat up then pushed herself out of the chair. "No, I told the owner she could keep them. Let's just go."

As they walked toward the exit, the young man who had been working behind the register skipped to catch up with them. "Miss Tate?"

They stopped and she turned to him. "Yes?"

"This was left for you." He handed her a sealed white envelope with *P. G. Tate* typed across the center then walked back behind the counter.

Gillian inhaled deeply then blew it out as she turned the envelope over and tore it open with her fingernail. "*What fresh hell is this?*" she said as she unfolded the single sheet of paper.

You Jezebel—

What peace, so long as your whoredoms
and witchcrafts are so many?

By her teaching she misleads my
servants into sexual immorality and
the eating of food sacrificed to
idols. I have given her time to
repent of her immorality, but she is
unwilling. Rev 2:20-21

The Sword of Michael the Archangel

Gillian raised her eyebrows. "Well, this is new. They've given me a nickname."

Sarah grabbed the letter out of her hand and scanned the type-written words on the page. "OK, Gillian, this has gone far enough. We have to go to the police with this."

"Why? And what exactly am I telling people to eat? Pork? Shellfish? The Bible sure is anti-good food."

"Don't you get it?" Sarah gripped Gillian by the upper arm and dragged her to the checkout counter. "Someone *left* this for you. One of those freaks was here."

"Oh, fuck!"

"Hey, Stuart," Sarah called to the kid behind the register, who stepped over to them. "Did you see who left this?"

He shook his head. "Sorry, you know it was a madhouse. I didn't even see it until I was shutting everything down. It was just sitting there. What is it?"

"It's nothing. Don't worry about it."

Sarah escorted her friend out of the bookstore. "This is getting serious. Come on. We went to the same Catholic high school. Don't you remember? I think Jezebel met with a pretty violent fate in the Bible."

With comprehension drawn on her face, Gillian's eyes widened. "Shit! I must have signed a book for one of those bastards. I smiled at him, maybe even shook his—or her—hand."

Jacob drove the car up in front of them, and they both got in. Once they were strapped in, Sarah asked him, "Do you know what happened to Jezebel in the Bible?"

"Uh, yeah. I think she was trampled to death by horses or something. Why?"

"Look at this." She handed her husband the letter. "Someone left this for Gillian during the book signing."

In the back seat, Gillian pulled off the red hair and the wig cap, and her long, dark hair tumbled free. "I don't quite foresee myself being trampled by horses in Manhattan."

Jacob handed the letter back to his wife and pulled the car away from the bookstore. He glanced at Gillian in the rearview mirror. "So what are you going to do about it?"

"Go home, go to bed, get back to work."

Chapter 2

Her body still on London time, Gillian awoke far earlier than she had set her alarm. She stared knives at the nightstand clock as if it were somehow responsible before getting up and making coffee. Then she stood with her mug in the living area, drinking coffee and peering out the terrace doors at the multi-million-dollar Manhattan view, purchased with the advance on the third novel in the *Thorns and Roses* ménage trilogy, which she had yet to begin.

Of the three spare bedrooms, she used the one facing south with its own doors out to the terrace as her office, frequently staring out at the City in search of the perfect word while completing the eighth and final draft of the second novel. She topped off her coffee, stumbled into the office, sat at her desk, and turned on her laptop. With her personal life in a tailspin, the pressure of promoting book two, and now the harassment of some zealot fringe group, not only had she not begun an outline—she didn't even have a title. The glare of the blank white page on the computer screen reflected in her eyes, the blinking cursor almost hypnotic. Eventually, she typed:

Thorns and Roses Trilogy
Book 1: Lying in Petals
Book 2: Pricked by Thorns

Book 3: **I**

The taunting blinking line of the cursor continued. And then…

The high-pitched whining from the faulty hot tub upstairs. A sign from above.

She picked up her cell phone and called Jack.

He answered with, "I hate you. *Uhhgh*. What kind of sick fuck calls at this hour?"

She smiled. "What's the matter with you?"

"I feel like Indira Gandhi. Too many shots from a Sikh."

"What?"

"I met this Sikh guy at the club last night, and he started buying us shots."

"I didn't think Sikhs drank."

"Well, this one's making up for all the Sikhs who don't."

"Hey, at least you're alive. Indira Gandhi was assassinated."

"She got off easy."

"So are you with him now?"

"No, we went our separate ways."

"What? He wasn't interested in your *Sikh heating missile*?" She laughed at her own play on words.

"Oh, you are hee-lar-ious." His dripping sarcasm emphasized each syllable. "Is there some purpose to this call?"

"Yeah, I've decided to take you up on your offer to use your parents' cabin."

"Really?"

"Are you sure they won't mind?"

"They never use it. Besides, they're on a cruise to Alaska or Antarctica or someplace old people go when they're retired and don't have anything better to do."

"I've got to get out of this apartment. Too many...annoyances."

"OK, hon. You're going to love it. It's on this gorgeous lake. Just come on over. I'll give you the key and directions."

Next she called Sarah. "Hey, what are you doing?"

"Just getting ready for church. What's up?"

"I'm going to go Upstate for a while."

"What? Where?"

"Jack's parents have a cabin in the Adirondacks. I'm going to go there, get away from cities, hate groups, ex-husbands, and hot tubs and try to write this novel before the deadline."

"Good. I'm glad you're getting away for a little while. Maybe things will have calmed down by the time you get back."

"I certainly hope so."

"How long do you think you'll be gone?"

"No idea. I'll be in touch and let you know how the novel is coming."

"OK. Good luck!"

"Thanks. I think I'm going to need it."

The squad car had already arrived on the scene when the detective from the 68th Precinct walked into the two-story stucco Bay Ridge home. The homeowners—Jacob and Sarah Falgert—sat on the couch with two patrolmen hovering near by, Mrs. Falgert in tears. The formal living room and the view of the dining room revealed nothing out of the ordinary, no indication of a robbery.

"Mr. Mrs. Falgert? I'm Detective Bennet. You reported a burglary?"

Falgert wrapped his arm around his wife's shoulders as she sniffed and brought a tissue to her nose. "Yes. My wife's office."

"This way, Detective," one of the patrolmen said and led him to the back of the house. The small room with a desk and a file cabinet and a clear view of the backyard lay in disarray—every file and desk drawer open and the contents tossed on the floor, a scanner/printer and a side table broken against the wall. "Looks like the perpetrator jimmied his way through here." The officer gestured toward the open backdoor, markings consistent with a crowbar along the split wood.

Bennet glanced out at the similar homes surrounding the house and backyard. "Broad daylight, and none of the neighbors saw anything?"

"No, sir."

Detective Bennet strode back into the living room and sat down in a chair adjacent to the sofa, taking out his notepad. "So, Mrs. Falgert, was your office the only one disturbed?" She nodded. "Was anything taken?"

"My l-laptop. My iPad. I think maybe some promotional material, but I'm not sure. They could have taken some papers, but how could I tell?"

"Are you employed outside your home?"

She shook her head. "No, just from my home office, but I spend a lot of time in the City with appointments and engagements."

"What is it you do exactly?" he asked, jotting down notes.

"I'm a l-literary agent."

"Literary agent? Not a typical target. Have you recently upset any clients or potential clients you may have rejected?"

"No, right now I only represent four authors, and they've all been with me for a while. They were all referrals. I don't even accept unsolicited queries."

"Where were you when this occurred?"

"We were at church," Jacob answered, "in Tribeca."

"What time did you leave home?"

"Just before ten."

"And you got back?"

"About an hour ago."

"That's a window of six hours. Are you usually gone this long on Sundays?"

"Yes," Sarah said. "After service, we get a bite to eat, then we go back for Bible study."

"So the perpetrator might have known your routine. Mr. Falgert, what do you do?"

"I'm an attorney here in Brooklyn."

"Do you have a home office?"

"Yes, but my partner and I practice out of our law

office a few miles from here."

"But your office here wasn't disturbed?"

"No."

"Mrs. Falgert, it looks like whoever did this was looking for something, especially considering the only thing taken was your laptop and your tablet. Do you know what that might have been?"

She shrugged, her eyebrows lifting with her shoulders. "Nothing. No idea."

The detective turned to Jacob. "Is it possible they thought your wife's office was yours? Any heated cases recently? Disgruntled clients or opposition?"

"I doubt it. I'm a tax attorney."

Sarah inhaled sharply with a squeal and covered her mouth with her hands, her eyes widening. "Gillian! They might have been looking for her address or something."

The detective set the tip of his pen on the pad, ready to write. "And who is Gillian?"

"She's one of my clients—P.G. Tate."

"You're P.G. Tate's agent? The author of that 'mommy porn'?"

"Yes, but that's not what we call it. It's erotic romance. She's been receiving threatening letters and emails from a group called the Sword of Michael the Archangel. One of them even showed up at a book signing yesterday." Sarah stood and walked over to a table just inside the front door, grabbing her messenger bag then returning to her place next to her husband. She took out the envelope and handed it to the detective. "We didn't see who it was, but he left this." Bennet pulled evidence gloves from his inside jacket pocket before taking the letter. "I'm afraid it has all of our fingerprints on it," Sarah said, "plus the boy's from the bookstore."

Detective Bennet scanned the letter. "How long has she been receiving these threats?"

Sarah explained how they had received harassing notes and emails after *Lying in Petals* came out but that the Sword of Michael group hadn't begun until shortly before the release of the second book. "What if they were looking for her address?"

Bennet called a patrolman over. "Get CSU over here. I want to get the office processed. And get an evidence bag for this," he said, pulling off a glove and handing it to him with the letter. "Have these threats been reported to the police?" he asked the couple.

"No," Jacob said. "We tried to get her to report them to the police, but she refused to take them seriously. She thought they were just 'nutjobs.'"

"Most of the time it is just some kooks. With your laptop and iPad, will they find her home address? If so, we should send a squad car over there."

"Of course they'd find her address, but fortunately she's not home. She just went somewhere Upstate today, and she won't be back for a while."

"Where Upstate?"

"Somewhere in the Adirondacks, but I'm not sure where."

"Sarah, if you know how to reach her," Jacob said, "you need to tell them."

"She's staying at her friend's parents' cabin, and there's no way to reach her. I got a voicemail from her while we were in church." She pulled out the phone and played the message on speaker.

> *Hey, it's me. I've been driving forEVER, but I'm almost there. Just stopped at this village or hamlet or whatever for provisions. I found out that there's no Internet or cell reception at the cabin, so I'll have to give you a call next time I come back here...so whenever I run out of wine. Talk to you later!*

"I don't even have a way to get in touch with her."

"Who's this friend, the one who lent her the cabin?"

"He's an author friend of hers. I've only met him a couple of times. His first name is Jack."

"No last name? Any way to reach him?"

"I don't know his real last name, but I'm friends with him on Facebook under his pen name. Patrick Fitzwilliam."

The detective wrote the name down and underlined it before coming to his feet, which prompted the couple to stand as well. "That should be enough to find him. CSU will be here soon to process the scene. If you think of anything else," he handed Sarah his card, "give me a call."

Chapter 3

Gillian stood in the cabin's claustrophobic kitchen, transported from an era of iceboxes and milkmen, unloading her meager purchases. She jumped at the hard knock on the door and turned to see a tall man through the glass panes. At the sight of the police uniform with standard-issue thick belt, gun, nightstick, and handcuffs, she gasped and flinched back, dropping the box of graham crackers in her hand. She tried several times to pull the door open for him without luck before noticing it swung outward, and she pushed it on its squeaky hinges.

"I-I didn't break in. I was invited to stay here."

His tone terse and authoritarian, he asked, "Are you Gillian Tate?" Mid-to-late forties with dark hair and a trim but muscular build, his strong jawline narrowed at a severe angle to his cleft chin. Gillian's image reflected in the dark sunglasses hiding his eyes.

"Y-yes. Is there a problem, Officer?"

"I'm the police chief, Sam Taylor. I got a call saying you've been receiving threatening letters and emails?" He pulled off his sunglasses to reveal dark, intense, deep-set eyes that took possession of all they surveilled. At that moment, they surveyed Gillian. His narrowed eyes traveled down the length of her voluptuous body—in jeans, a faded Knicks t-shirt, and a thick, gray sweater—then up to her face, free of make-up and framed in dark loose curls.

She leaned back against the door with her hands behind her back, averting her gaze under his appraisal, a hint of pink rising in her cheeks and the beginnings of a smile twitching on her lips. "Well, I'd say more harassing than threatening."

"I'm here to check on you, make sure you're all right."

"They sent the police chief? I'm honored!" The corners of her mouth rose as she met his dark eyes.

"I, uh, it wasn't out of my way. I have a cabin down by the road to town." He peered over his shoulder in that direction. "Rent it to tourists during the summer, but I stay there a lot during the off season."

"I don't blame you. It's beautiful up here on the lake, with the trees changing colors. I can't believe this is considered the off-season."

"I mainly stay here to maintain a presence, keep an eye on the vacant cabins—teenagers, transients." With his hands on his hips, he turned toward the lake where, mirrored in the still water, the setting sun lit the trees on fire. "We had a long summer, so the leaves peaked late," he said, focusing on anything besides Gillian Tate. "You're lucky. Usually after Columbus Day, the colors are gone, all the leaves are brown."

"And the sky is gray?" She raised her eyebrows, and he looked at his shoes then finally back to her with a grin. "Do you mind coming in? I'm getting tired of holding this door."

He grabbed the door as she walked in, but as it squeaked and clanked behind him, he only stepped just inside the kitchen while she rescued the graham crackers, setting them on the counter before leaning against the sink. She glanced back at him, but when she met his gaze, they both looked away. Once shut off from the trees and the lake and the cool, rustling wind, in the cloister of the tiny kitchen as the orange light poured through the windows, the air thickened between them as dense as buttercream frosting.

After several seconds of standing in silence and avoiding eye contact, Gillian took a deep breath and returned to her task of unloading the groceries with her back to him. "Would you like a glass of wine? I'm afraid that's all I have right now. Oh, but you're 'on the job,' aren't you? Do you want me to make coffee?"

"To be frank, I'm off duty; but no, thank you."

"Why do you have to be Frank? Do you have to be Frank to be off duty?" She flashed a grin at him as she stepped to the living room with a bottle of wine in each hand. "You don't like being Sam Taylor?"

"What?"

"Is it short for Samuel?"

"Well, uh, yeah." Perplexion creased between his eyes as they followed her movements around the shrinking kitchen.

"I like the name Samuel. It means something like 'God hears you,' El, of course, meaning God."

"How long have you been here? I haven't seen you in town before."

"I, uh, actually just arrived. What's going on out

there? Looks like your little hamlet is done up for a festival or a holiday or something."

"Um, yeah. You're just in time. Today's the last night of Oktoberfest."

"Oktoberfest? Here?"

"Yeah, it's mainly for the locals, those who don't want to make the trip to Lake Placid. You should come check it out." He glimpsed up at the bottles of wine on the table. "But I guess you're not much of a beer drinker."

She rolled her eyes up at him with a crooked smile. "Well, I have been to college. Of course I drink beer, but I don't know how festive I am. I'm dealing with monster jetlag. I need to get some rest so I can get some work done. Plus, I won't know anyone there."

"I'll be there. In an official capacity, technically off-duty, but I want to be there just to, you know."

Her eyebrows lifted when she glanced at him. "Maintain a presence?"

He smiled at her. "Pretty much."

"Still, as much as I appreciate the power of your presence, I wouldn't exactly say I know you, Chief Taylor."

"We could change that."

She bit her bottom lip as color rose in her face, and she focused on her groceries.

"You don't seem concerned about these threatening letters," Taylor said.

"Why should I be? I'm not intimidated by *you*, coming here with your Batman belt and your gun and handcuffs." Her eyes flared with humor and a glint of something more.

"Yes, but I'm an officer of the law."

She laughed. "Exactly my point."

"So if I don't make you nervous, does that mean you always ramble on about the etymology of the name of everyone you meet?"

"Oooh—" Her brows drew together as she pursed her lips on the extended syllable, glancing over her shoulder at him. "*Etymology*. Impressive!"

"I went to college, too. Not all us backwoods law officers are ignorant hicks."

"Glad to hear it. And, yes, to answer your question, I do. I am fascinated with etymology." Then she added, while shaking a canned good at him, "And I wasn't rambling."

"If you say so." But hopeful incredulity had exposed his deep dimples and the fine lines in the corners of his eyes.

"Why would I let a few anonymous messages get to me? OK, so, who asked you to come check on me? Sarah? Jack?"

"No, it was a New York City police detective."

The blood and smile draining from her face, she stopped and turned to him, squeezing the bag of marshmallows in her hand. "A detective. Did something happen? Is everything OK?"

"Someone broke into the home of, uh, Mr. and Mrs. Falgert. You know them? Tossed the place apart, stole her laptop."

"Oh, my god! Is Sarah all right?"

"Yes, she and her husband weren't home at the time."

She released an extended breath. "That's a relief.

Shit. I can't even call her from up here. And they think it's related to the threats against me?"

"They aren't sure, but they don't want to rule anything out in case the person, or persons, sending you these messages was trying to get your address or find out where you are."

She set the marshmallows on the counter next to the graham crackers. "Do you mind if *I* have some wine?"

"Not at all." He ventured a step away from the door. "In fact, I think I *will* join you."

"Did…did they get my home address?" She walked into the constricted living area where several wine bottles stood in formation on the small dining table like the infantry. After grabbing one at random, she rummaged through the kitchen drawers before finding a corkscrew. Even setting the bottle on the crowded kitchen counter, her shaking hands struggled to open it.

"Yes, but no information on where you're staying up here on the lake." Taylor walked up beside her and wrapped his hand around hers. "Here." He pulled her hand off the bottle and took the corkscrew. "Let me help you with that before you hurt yourself."

"Ho-how did you find me?"

"NYPD spoke with someone called Patrick Fitzwilliam or Michael Fitzpatrick or something."

"That's Jack. This is his parents' cabin." As he twisted out the cork, she opened cabinets and returned with two juice glasses. "Couldn't find any wine glasses, but," she shrugged, "this is what they use in Italy."

He filled one of the glasses three-quarters full then

handed it to her, and she took several swallows as he poured half a glass for himself. "Miss Tate—or is it Mrs.?"

"Uh, just call me Gillian."

"Maybe you should sit down, Gillian. You seem upset."

"No, I'll be OK." She drank again then brought her glass and the bottle of wine to the table before turning back to the shopping bags. "It was a long drive up here, and I'm really tired. I just hope the break-in has nothing to do with those wackjobs. I'll feel terrible if this happened because I didn't take it seriously." She placed a pack of hotdogs in the ancient single-door refrigerator/freezer in desperate need of defrosting.

"So that's not why you're up here? To get away from the people threatening you?"

"No, I came up here to…get away from everything, really, try to get some work done."

"Are you alone? I mean, is anyone staying up here with you?"

With no pantry to speak of, she began moving her canned goods to the top of the refrigerator. "Nope. Just little old me."

"No…boyfriend or…" He drank from his juice glass then licked his lips. "*Mr.* Tate?"

"Yes, there is a Mr. Tate." Taylor cast his eyes downward until she said, "He's probably framing our divorce decree as we speak."

He smiled and took another sip of wine as he watched her curvaceous figure stretching to put the groceries away. "I'm sorry," he said, but his voice conveyed no regret.

"And you?" she asked with a quick glance in his direction. "Is there a *Mrs.* Police Chief?" When she turned, she knocked a few cans onto the floor and dropped the two in her hands. She started to crouch down to get them, but Taylor beat her to it.

"Not for a long, long time," he said as he passed her the cans. Then he began reading the labels aloud as he handed them to her. "Beef stew, ravioli. Are these *canned* tamales? *This* is what you brought up here to eat?"

"I...I haven't been camping since I was a Girl Scout."

"I guess that accounts for your marshmallows and chocolate bars."

"For s'mores."

"Yes, I'm familiar with them. You know, I wouldn't call this camping. You aren't exactly roughing it here. You *can* cook. It's a fully-equipped cabin with a stove and oven and even running water."

"I did bring hotdogs."

"*Canned* chili?"

She grabbed the can out of his hand. "That's for the hotdogs!" When he looked back at her, a grin crinkled his eyes. "Coming up here was a spur-of-the-moment decision," she said. "I wasn't sure what to bring."

"You're in no short supply of wine."

"Was there something else you wanted, Chief Taylor, or are you just hanging around here to make fun of my groceries?" She set the can of chili on the table, exchanging it for her glass of wine.

"No, I'm sorry, Miss Tate," he said, but the smile on his lips negated the apology. "I wanted to ask you what these threats are all about, who is harassing you and why."

"Some fringe group. They don't like what I write."

"Are you a journalist or something?"

"They didn't tell you who I am?" He responded only with a short jerk of his head and wrinkling his brows together. "Have you heard of *P.G. Tate*?"

"The woman who writes those kinky novels? Wait. That's not you."

"Yes...Why? Is that so hard to believe?"

"You just don't seem like the type."

She splashed more wine into her glass and leaned back against the table. "Sorry to disappoint you. I left my dominatrix catsuit and flogger at home."

"I'm surprised, but..." Again, his eyes traced her curves. "I'm definitely not disappointed."

Heat tinted her cheeks. "What's so surprising?"

"I just wouldn't expect a Girl Scout..."

"You wouldn't expect a Girl Scout to grow up and write erotic romance novels?"

"No. Well, yes. I mean, it's just, aren't your books about three-ways and BDSM?"

"Yes. I mean, not S and M so much; mainly the BDS part."

He squinted at her. "You just seem so...normal."

"*Ugh!*" She rolled her eyes. "Why wouldn't I be? In case you don't know, the books have done quite well, so evidently there are a lot of 'normal' women who enjoy having sexual fantasies. The psychos who are harassing me—are *they* the 'normal' ones?"

He took the two steps required to stand a few inches in front of her, sincerity in his eyes this time when he apologized, his deep voice low and soothing. "Hey, I'm sorry. You're right. I shouldn't have said that, especially with what happened with your friend. I know this must be disturbing."

Without looking back, she set her glass on the table behind her and raised her head to meet his penetrating stare, the wine doing nothing to abate the quickening of her shallow breaths. "You know, now I do feel kind of intimidated by your Batman belt."

His gaze flicked down to her mouth then back to her eyes. He raised one hand but stopped short of touching her face, instead lifting his other and grasping her shoulders. "To be completely fra- *honest*, I've never given *P.G. Tate* much thought. Kind of hard to escape knowing who she is, with all the publicity surrounding her, I mean, *your* books."

"Right. I know. I've seen the headlines. 'P.G. Rated X.'"

"I just had this image of some fashionable, shallow, pretentious Manhattanite."

"Well, actually, I *am* trying."

Pulsations fluttered rapidly through their veins as the heated attraction held her in his stare. She flushed and shuddered under the weight of his stare.

"What…what is it?" Her soft voice fluttered out with her breath.

He swallowed, his eyes caressing her face as his hands could not. "I was just thinking, I wish we hadn't just met."

"That's not a very nice thing to say."

"No, I wish we hadn't *just* met. And under these circumstances." His eyes landed on her mouth, and her cheeks bloomed as she licked her lips. With a final squeeze on her tight shoulder muscles, he said, "How about dinner to welcome you to the neighborhood. Let me fix you a *real* home cooked meal—you know, not out of a can—tomorrow night? No Batman belt, I promise."

She scraped her top teeth across her bottom lip. "Well, that's a shame."

With a hitch in his breath, he dropped his hands to his sides. "What do you say? Six o'clock all right?"

"So would this fall under the 'serve' part of 'To serve and protect'?"

"I'd say both since I'm protecting you from that so-called food you have in there."

"Can I bring anything?"

"You sure you don't have that catsuit?"

"Not hardly," she said with a giggle in her voice. "You really haven't read my books?"

He puffed out his cheeks and blew. "I haven't. Don't take it personally."

A sly smirk tweaking her lips, she walked into the other room and returned with a copy of *Lying in Petals*. She set it down on the table with a pen and focused on the inscription. "I don't think you would like the second in the series, but maybe this one..." She closed it and handed it to him, his fingers sliding across hers as he accepted, his piercing dark eyes meeting hers.

"Here's my card," he said as he handed it to her. "Come by the station if you need anything."

She studied it. "Thanks, I will, Police Chief Sam Taylor."

"And think about coming to the fest tonight, since you are all alone. We have a troupe of slap dancers coming."

"Slap dancers? Is that like break dancers?"

He chuckled. "No, the *schuhplattler*. It's a Bavarian folk dance. They slap their knees and the bottom of their shoes..."

She scrunched her nose and eyebrows as her upper lip curled. "Uhhhh...as tempting as that sounds, I think I'm going to pass." She walked with him through the tiny kitchen to the door. "Six tomorrow?"

"Last cabin before the turnoff. Probably the only one with lights on."

"I'll see you then."

He had parked several yards from the cabin and glanced back at it a few times, a grin curving his mouth as she watched him walk away. When he opened his squad car door, the interior light came on. He turned the book to her inscription.

> To Chief Taylor~
> There's s'mores where this came from.
>   Gillian

His smile punctuated with an extra beat of his heart, he closed the car door and drove away.

Chapter 4

Standing in the kitchen in her bathrobe, Gillian fought with the hand-crank can opener until she finally managed to lift the lid off the ravioli. She leaned against the counter and ate it straight out of the can with a spoon, drinking wine out of a juice glass. With each bite, her gaze wandered up at the ceiling and around the kitchen. She smiled when her eyes landed on the can of tamales on top of the refrigerator, and she tapped her spoon on her bottom lip. Setting her ravioli on the counter, she picked up Chief Taylor's business card and scanned it before sticking the corner between her two front teeth.

With the grin and the card still adorning her mouth, her eyes flickered back and forth and around, never focusing on anything, until she set the card down by the ravioli and picked up the can. She opened the cabinet under the sink, which housed the garbage can, but then closed it and stuck the ravioli in the refrigerator, spoon and all. After finishing off her glass of wine, she walked with purpose toward the bedroom, shedding her robe along the way.

On the road to town, she drove past the police

chief's dimly-lit cabin, but his cruiser wasn't on the driveway. She exhaled a long, rattled breath through narrowed lips as she made the turn.

Even as she eased into a parking place, the sounds of accordions and zithers seeped into her car. She turned off the engine and dug her cellphone out from her purse. The home page lit up a message, ten percent of battery remaining, which she dismissed before calling Sarah. The call rolled straight to voicemail, but before Gillian could leave a message, her phone died in her hand.

"How was that ten percent!" she said to the black screen. She turned on the dome light and searched the storage areas under the console and the arm rest but came up empty-handed. "Idiot, idiot, idiot." She shook her head with a sigh and tossed the useless rectangle of glass and plastic onto the passenger seat and grappled her way out of the vehicle.

Gillian followed the lights and polka music to the Oktoberfest gathering. She eased her way through the rapidly-thinning crowd, most dressed in dirndls or lederhosen and almost all a full two decades older than she, aside from a few dozen teenagers on the carnival rides set off from the rest of the spectacle.

Yodelers performed on a stage set up near the refreshment stands, so she ordered a beer and an oversized pretzel, along with a cheese spread called *obatzda*, and hustled to the town square on the other side where well-rehearsed septuagenarians moved with precision through the folk dance accompanied by an accordion and some unseen *boom-pah boom-pah* instruments. She settled in at a table with a decent view, and a grin lightened her face as she drank her beer and dipped the pretzel into the buttery-cheesy mush, despite her occasional glance around never landing on that familiar face or uniform.

She joined in the applause and cheers when the polka ended as the dancers made their bows, but then the calls of "s*chuhplattler*" and "slap dancers" had everyone scattering toward the stage, and she pushed herself up to join them, tossing the remnants of her food in a receptacle but bringing her beer along.

The crowd closed in on the stage as the performance began, and from the rear of the audience, she laughed as the men did indeed dance as Chief Taylor had predicted, slapping their thighs and feet. After a few minutes, she covered her yawn with her hand and blinked back her fatigue.

"I hope you aren't bored."

She flinched under the depth of the voice behind her, and a chill shivered up her spine when his hot breath brushed her cool neck. "Oh, no, not at all. I'm just tired."

"So what do you think?"

She twisted her neck to meet the Chief's black eyes. "They, uh, kind of remind me of the puppet show from *The Sound of Music*," she said, her small, tentative smile a mirror of his own. "In fact, the whole festival reminds me of that."

"Well, that takes place in Austria, and Austria was once part of Bavaria."

They both turned to face one another, eyes and grins glittering in the festival lights. "You mean it's not?"

"Oh, no!" He shook his head and brought his brows together in exaggerated solemnity. "Not since 976 when Duke Henry the Quarrelsome lost a revolt that led to the creation of Austria."

She laughed. "You're kidding, right? *Henry the Quarrelsome*? You're making that up."

He held up three fingers. "Scout's honor. As police chief, I have a duty to know these things. Just ask me about Pépin the Hunchback sometime."

She giggled and took a sip from her cup. "What about Prince Dennis the Menacing?"

"No, but I have heard of Hagar the Horrible." Without his gun and belt, his uniform hung on his trim physique without the stiffness of his office. His muscles had loosened, too; and although he smiled at her as often as at their first meeting, his relaxed manner allowed him not to look away.

"Pépin the Hunchback…You're lucky I don't have Internet so I could Google your ass."

"I doubt you'll find my ass, but you will find Pépin and Henry—I promise you that. I minored in history. Every once in a while it comes in handy."

"So was Henry truly quarrelsome?"

"I'd say so. He was always instigating some kind of revolt. He even tried kidnapping his three year-old cousin."

She chuckled. "That's terrible!"

"Don't worry. The cousin went on to become emperor of Rome and got into a turf battle over who should be pope."

"Oh, well, that's a relief. Now I'll be able to sleep tonight."

They fell quiet as the slap dancers continued in the background, and Taylor's smile faded as his stare traced her face. "I'm glad you changed your mind. About coming to the festival."

She averted her eyes down to her lukewarm beer. "I, uh, I came down to get a signal to try to call Sarah…Sarah Falgert?...but I hadn't charged my phone and I stupidly must have left my car charger in New York."

He cast his gaze down her form. "You look very pretty in that dress. I'm sure Mrs. Falgert would have appreciated it."

She lifted her eyes to his and bit the bottom lip of her shy smile but said nothing.

"Can I get you another beer? What are you drinking?"

"Lowenbrau. I didn't even know they still made this stuff. But no, thanks, I'm already so exhausted. Another beer would probably knock me on my ass."

"I would definitely have to Google that."

The slap dancers finished their act, and Gillian and Taylor turned toward the stage to join in the applause.

"How'd you like them?" he asked.

"That was definitely something to see, but I really enjoyed watching the folk dancers in the town square. That looked like it would be fun."

Taking the cup away from her, he grasped her cool fingers in his warm hand. "Come on. They'll be starting again in a few minutes. Let's join them."

He tugged her forward, but she resisted, eyes wide and shaking her head. "I…No, no, I don't know how to polka or whatever they're doing. The only polka I know is the chicken dance."

He sniffed out a laugh. "It's all right. I'll help you."
When she held her ground, he turned to face her with a
short shrug. "Just tell me: Do you want to polka?"

She narrowed her eyes and suppressed a laugh. "I
think that might be the strangest question anyone has
ever asked me."

"I doubt that, coming from *the* P.G. Tate." He
dragged her on and threw her cup in the trash along the
away. "You're familiar with square dancing?"

"No, I've never square danced either."

"Yes, but you are familiar with it, right? You've
seen it before, on TV or movies?"

"Well, yes, but I—"

"Many of the dance moves are similar, except like a
waltz. Watch the others, and just follow their lead."

"But-but I'm not dressed appropriately. I need an
apron or a kerchief or something."

"And I'll be the only one in a police uniform.
C'mon. I'll be dancing with the prettiest girl here."

"Ha. That's just because every other woman here is
old enough to be your mother. I didn't know this was a
town of retirees."

"It's just getting late on a Sunday night. Most
people have work in the morning or kids to get ready
for school. It wouldn't have mattered." He helped her
off with her sweater and set it on a chair with her
purse. "I'd say you're the prettiest girl in New York."

"Oh, I see. Using flattery to get your way."

"It's not flattery when it's true."

"Uh-huh. You think my purse is safe there?"

"You're with the police chief. No one would dare.

Besides, you really think this town of retirees is going to steal it?"

"Well, what about my sweater. I'll be cold."

"Not for long."

They joined the end of the line behind eight other couples, and Gillian shook her head. "I can't believe I'm doing this."

"Just follow along. I'll help you."

The music began, and he took her into a ballroom pose, a spark igniting between them when he placed his hand on her back. "Oh! Must be static electricity."

"Must be." He smiled and they followed the other couples.

They waltzed around in a circle in the center of the town square, and as the music concluded, he turned her under his left arm.

With eyes wide and sparkling, she said, "Well, that wasn't hard."

"We're just getting started. Now we all join hands." After a moment's confusion as the music began again, she glimpsed the outstretched arm of the elderly gentleman to her right and held hands with both him and Taylor. Taylor leaned down and spoke against her ear. "We step to the left….And now to the right."

She shuffled her feet for a beat behind the others as they changed directions, and she couldn't suppress a giggle. "I'm terrible!"

"You're fine. See you in a minute."

"Wait—What?" But he had already handed her off to the older man to their left, and then the next lederhosen-clad gentleman took her hand, and so on as they progressed around the circle of dancers.

Once she reached Taylor again, he said, "I'm going to turn you," a split second before he twirled her under his right arm even as the next man extended his left hand and spun her in the other direction.

With gaping eyes, she puffed out her rosy cheeks and blew out a weary breath before continuing on, smiling at each of her grinning partners. Once she had managed to polka around the circle without an "Oops!" or "Other hand, dear" or stepping on any arthritic feet, the dance changed again; and Taylor linked their elbows as they turned around in place.

He kept his smiling face turned to hers as he asked, "Having fun?" but before she could answer, they were on to the next dancers.

When the music paused, he stood at her left. "Yes," she said. "I'm having fun."

"Good."

"But how long does this go on?"

He chuckled, raising his arms as the music started up again, and he stepped forward to join hands with the other men. Gillian froze, motionless while watching them stomp around as the cheery-faced women stood in place with hands on hips, twisting side to side in time with the polka.

As the men backed up, the women stepped forward, clasping hands, and she mimicked their ring-around-the-rosies. When the stomping men came forward again, Taylor and a man on her right brought their arms over her head and joined hands across her chest. She gasped, her head jerking up to Taylor's grinning face when his arm brushed her breast.

"Oops," he said with a wink as he and the other

men raised their linked hands over the heads of the women.

Then the men wove themselves into the circle by coming up under the linked arms of the women. Gillian shrieked her surprise and pulled away, releasing the hands of the ladies on either side, breaking the ring, and leaving Taylor and the other man with no *Fräulein* between them. The dancers quickly adapted when Taylor bowed out to follow Gillian.

Her squeals had disintegrated into giggles as Taylor wrapped his arm around her back, his hand curling around to cradle her elbow while he escorted her away from the square.

"Are you all right?" A hint of humor hitched his voice, dimples cutting hard ridges around his mouth. "What happened?"

Her laughter forced her forward for a few seconds, but she managed to quell it enough to straighten, wipe the tears forming at the corners of her eyes, and speak. "I just wasn't expecting…" She turned to face him, his hand sliding around her back before alighting on her other arm. "When you—both of you—came under my arms, I was surprised, is all. I mean, that's a far cry from the chicken dance!"

"I hope you enjoyed yourself, at least."

"Definitely, but every time I figured out what we were supposed to be doing, it would change. It really wasn't hard. I think I just need a pneumonic to remember. Circle to the left, circle to the right, link elbows, twirl, men forward, women forward, then men scare the crap out of the women."

He laughed. "That's pretty close. Of course, it's not over yet."

The polka music played on, and creases formed over her nose. "How long *is* that dance anyway?"

"Seriously, I think you did extremely well for your first polka. It's not like you've got a lot of experience with Bavarian folk dances."

She smiled up at him with a tilt of her head and brows raised. "I'll have you know I do know the Ländler."

"The Ländler? You really are full of surprises." He hadn't removed his hand, nor had she stepped out of his reach, and he began to move his thumb and fingers in circles on her upper arm. "How did you come to learn that?"

"From *The Sound of Music*."

"Now that's the second time you've mentioned that film in the last hour."

She shrugged her shoulders forward and crossed her arms. "What can I say? It's probably my favorite movie?"

"That's it!" He removed his hand from her to raise both palms in protest. Now I know you're lying."

"Lying!"

"There is no way you are P.G. Tate if your favorite movie is *The Sound of Music*."

"Well, it was when I was a kid. I still like it, but now I fast-forward through most of the songs."

He braced his hands on his hips and shook his head. "Doesn't that kind of defeat the purpose of the *sounds* of music?"

"I...uh..." she said, her smile tingling her tone. "I

guess I've just outgrown most of them, but I never fast-forward through the Ländler scene."

"As much as I hate to admit it, I don't think I've seen the movie quite as many times as you. When is the Ländler scene?"

"Oh, come on! When the Captain and Maria dance together, and they realize…well, it's a very romantic scene."

"Oh, right. Yeah, I remember it now."

"My sister and I used to practice it together until we had it memorized, but since she was older, I always had to be the Captain."

"Well, Captain." He held his hand out to her. "Shall we?"

She took his offered hand even as skeptical curiosity narrowed her eyes. "Shall we what?"

"The Ländler."

"Oh, no." She tried to pull her hand free, but he grasped her fingers. "I think I've brought enough attention to myself by dancing with every seventy year-old man in town in the middle of the square."

"You might be surprised that that wasn't even a fraction of the men over seventy here, but this is not a group dance." He stepped around, placing his hand on the small of her back, and nudged her toward the bandstand. "This time I won't have to hand you off."

"What?"

"We'll let them do their thing, and we'll go over there." He nodded in the direction of an adjoining parking area. When they reached the musicians, he said to the zither player, "Could you do a Ländler next?" After receiving a nod of assent, he led her to the empty, dimly-lit parking lot.

"I have never met any man who likes to dance as much as you do. In fact, I've never met a man who likes to dance—a straight man, that is."

"Oh, didn't you know? I'm the gay police chief of the Adirondacks."

"If that's the case, you would have preferred my second book; but for some reason, I doubt that very seriously."

"Good," he said, his voice deep and gruff as they came to a halt and faced each other. "I don't always like to dance. It depends on the inducements of the partner."

She blushed but said, "I don't know how I could possibly stand a chance with all those lovely ladies with their silver hair."

"Well, they are already partnered, so you are stuck with me. We can do a practice run while we wait for the Ländler to begin. First, I bow—"

"And I curtsey." After doing so, he took her hand. "And then we take a little walk," she said.

After a few steps, he attempted to turn her while she tried to pull him forward, and they both lost their balance and collided.

"What are you doing?" they said in unison. "The Ländler."

He squinted at her. "What Ländler are you doing?"

"In the movie, they take a little walk and then step-hop, step-hop."

"Well, I hate to disillusion you, sweetheart, but that's not the Ländler."

"It isn't?"

"I think they might have just incorporated some of the moves into the choreography."

"My sister would be heartbroken. After all those hours of practice." She turned to walk away.

"Where are you going?"

"I thought I knew it, but I guess I don't."

He grasped her shoulder and walked around to face her, gripping her with his intense stare. "You don't have to know it."

"Of course I do. I won't know what to do."

"You just have to let me lead. Do you think you could follow me, let me lead for a change, Captain?"

Her gaze dropped as she stood silent for a moment then spoke in a hushed tone. "I've been *leading* almost all my life."

"Do you think you're ready to let someone else take the lead? I won't let you fall."

She looked up and met his eyes. "Yes. Very much so."

In the meantime, the polka had ended, and a muffled announcement drifted into the parking lot where they stood under a streetlight. He took both her hands, and zither music began. "This is it. Just follow my lead."

She nodded then curtsied as he bowed. He took her hand as they stepped in time with the music, and he turned her three times. Then he took her other hand and he swung their arms to the rhythm.

"From now on," he said, "I'll hold onto both of your hands. I won't let go."

She nodded, and he turned her slowly under his right arm, their hands linked behind her back and in front of him, their bodies facing opposite directions, but his eyes still holding hers. He repeated the turn twice to return them to the same position, held together in their locked arms.

Another turn and they followed the steps in the same direction, but he never spoke again, no more instructions, only smiled as he guided her through the dance.

The rhythm of the zither music sped up, and he twirled her four times in quick succession, bringing their right arms around her waist, their sides flush together as they turned in opposite directions and stared at each other through the ring formed over their heads by their joined left hands.

Then as he began the next set of turns to reverse their positions, her eyes fluttered, and she fell back against his chest, his arms still around her waist although her grip had slackened.

"Gillian?" He turned her enough to see her ashen face and patted her cheek gently as her eyes blinked open. "Are you OK?"

She stood up straight, releasing herself from the comfort of his arms and raising a hand to her temple. "All the twirling. I got so dizzy. I...I'm sorry."

"Don't apologize. I've never had a woman swoon in my arms before. How much Lowenbrau did you have?"

She glanced up and met his grin. "You tossed out my only one. I'm just exhausted. It's really late."

"It's not even ten."

"Not in London. I told you I have terrible jetlag."

"And I told you I wouldn't let you fall."

"Yes. You did."

"Your face is all red."

"Is it? I don't suppose I'm used to dancing." She smiled, but, still unsteady on her feet, her eyelids drifted down, and he caught her against him.

"Come on. I better drive you home."

"But I have my car."

"We'll take your car. I'll walk back to my cabin and have one of the guys from the station pick me up in the morning."

"It's only three miles. I don't want you to—"

"There's no argument. Here's another time you're going to let me lead. Now let's go find out if someone stole your purse and sweater," he said, eliciting a chuckle. "So were you cold?"

"No, not at all. You were right. And thank you. For making me dance."

"We'll have to finish another time. You were dancing beautifully."

"You are an excellent leader."

"Only for someone willing to follow."

Trying to keep the yawning Gillian awake on the short drive, he asked her about how close she and her sister had been.

"She's more than four years older, but we were both chunky teens. She didn't have a whole lot of friends, so I think I got her attention by default. Plus, she could boss me around. She blossomed when she went to Berkeley for college—gorgeous and thin, even living in Italy with all that amazing food."

"And how about you? When did you blossom?"

She sniffed. "I'm still waiting."

"What are you talking about? You're beautiful and successful and have international popularity."

"I lost most of the baby fat by senior year, but I've always been heavy."

He took his eyes off the road just long enough to glance at her. "You're insane. You are not heavy. You're—"

"Pleasantly plump."

He shook his head. "I was going to say voluptuous. Lush. Sensuous. Not like those bony anorexics or workout freaks that are all hard muscle. When we danced tonight, I knew I was holding a woman in my arms."

She turned to stare out the passenger window, her blush hidden by the dark but not her shy smile.

"How about you?" she asked. "Were you close to your family?"

"Well, to give you a hint, I accepted a baseball scholarship at Seattle University. I wasn't good enough for any of the bigger programs; and at the time, I just wanted to get as far away from my father as possible. We were constantly butting heads. He was so domineering."

"I understand. My sister and I could never satisfy our parents. We were both terrible disappointments to them, and it only got worse for me after Catherine left."

"My father and I eventually made our peace, but it was really more a state of détente. At least it pleased my mother."

After seeing Gillian safely to her cabin, finalizing their plans for her "welcome" dinner, and walking home, Taylor sat on the end of his couch by the lamp table with reading glasses perched near the end of his nose and his feet on the coffee table, a novel by P.G. Tate in his hands. In the middle of the fourth chapter, his eyebrows rose, and he turned the book over to see the photo of the author, the glammed-up redhead bearing little resemblance to the luscious woman with dark curls he had held in his arms as they danced just hours before.

He shook his head and snickered as he returned to the prose. "Whew," he said, ignoring the tightness growing in his jeans.

Meanwhile, in a cabin just under a mile down the lake, after a shower Gillian had gained a second wind and sat in bed drinking wine, a notebook on her lap and a pen in hand. She smiled and bit her bottom lip as she began jotting notes for the outline of her new novel: "likes to dance; intense eyes; dark hair; trim, muscular build; strong jaw line narrowing at a severe angle to his cleft chin."

Chapter 5

The door of the screened-in front porch clattered shut behind Gillian, so before she could knock, Chief Taylor had opened the house door and popped his head out. She walked toward him carrying a bottle of wine in one hand and a shopping bag in the other, her hair loose around her shoulders, wearing a dark blue dress with a tiny floral print that fell below her knees, a long sweater that dropped even lower, tennis shoes, and a small smile that shown more in her eyes than on her lips.

"Hi there," he said as he watched her approach.

"Hey."

"I didn't hear you drive up." He took the bag and wine from her and stepped back to let her by. "What's all this?"

"Wine and stuff in case you'd like s'mores. I didn't drive; I walked." She squeezed past him and his woodsy scent of pine and leather into the living room, redolent with tomato sauce and Italian spices. "Something smells good."

"Walked? That's almost a mile."

"You walked here last night." She followed as he

strode into the kitchen, slightly larger than the one in her cabin. "I'm from Manhattan. I walk all the time. Besides, it's such a beautiful night along the lake."

"Yeah, but it's getting dark, and you've been receiving threats from some hate group."

"You said yourself they don't know where I am."

"Do you even have a flashlight?"

"Thanks again for driving me home last night."

"My pleasure. You had a good time?"

"Oh, absolutely. Sorry about my jetlag. I slept almost all day."

"Good. I think you needed it."

"Nice cabin you have here."

"Thanks. Not too different from yours."

She scanned the living room and off-set kitchen. "Quite a bit larger…and size does matter."

He glanced at her with a crooked smile. "I'd already opened a bottle of wine." He poured the deep, crimson Chianti into a long-stemmed tapered glass. "If you don't mind, we'll save yours for later."

"Oooh, actual wine glasses," she said, accepting it from him. As he poured one for himself, she took in his tall, muscular form dressed in tight jeans and a blue plaid shirt, the top few buttons open to expose a hint of hair on his chest. "I've been wondering what you looked like out of uniform."

His eyebrows bounced up with his short laugh, then he turned to clink their glasses together while keeping his eyes on hers. "Cheers, and welcome to the neighborhood."

"Thank you, Chief Taylor."

"Just Sam. I *am* out of uniform."

They sipped the robust wine, and she rolled it around in her mouth before swallowing then licking the center of her lips with the tip of her tongue. "Well, *Sam*, can I ask you something? Is this just a casual, 'welcome to the neighborhood' dinner, or is this a date?"

"What do you want it to be?"

Her gaze fell onto his open shirt then up to his mouth and back to his eyes before she took another sip from her glass. "Can I decide afterwards?"

Raising his hand to her face, he rubbed his thumb across her bottom lip to wipe away the non-existent drop of wine there, her shallow, rapid breaths against his skin. "Of course." Then he turned back to the oven and grabbed a hotpad. "You mentioned visiting your sister in Italy. I hope you like lasagna."

"Lasagna? Impressive. You really *do* know how to cook."

With a sheepish grin, he pulled a large foil pan out of the oven, replacing it with a loaf of Italian bread. "Uh, actually, turned out I didn't have much time after work, so I got this from an Italian restaurant in town. I suppose the more gentlemanly thing to do would have been to take you there."

"But then this would definitely be a date."

"Or maybe I'm just not a gentleman." He glanced at her with teasing eyes as he drank from his glass. "It's still homemade, by them. And it's much better than a can of ravioli."

"I don't know. That ravioli was pretty good last night."

"You really ate that?"

"Sure. And half a pretzel at the fest. Why? Did you have something better?"

"Uh, yes. I…" He grabbed a large plastic bowl of salad out of the refrigerator and pulled off the lid before facing her again. "I read a few chapters of your book."

"Oh, no!" She turned away, covering her blush with her hand. "You actually read it?"

"If you didn't want me to read it, why'd you give it to me?"

"Because I really didn't expect you to read a romance novel!"

He laughed and, with one hand between her shoulder blades and the other carrying the salad, led her to the table. "Come here. Sit down. I admit, it is my first romance novel, but I enjoyed what I read." His knuckles skimmed down her arms sending a shudder down her back as he helped her shrug out of her sweater. He laid it over a chair before pulling out the one close to his at the small oak table where he had set their places, a candle lit in the center.

"Now I'm going to be sitting here all night wondering what's going on in your head."

"You don't have to wonder. I'll tell you."

"I'm afraid to ask."

"First of all," he said, standing behind her with an advantageous view of her décolletage as he pushed her chair under the table, "I'm thinking how pretty you look in that dress." He walked back to the kitchen and pulled the bread from the oven, dropping it into a basket. "As for the book, I think you write very well."

"Even erotica can be well-written."

"I'm already thinking this isn't going to work out for Harry."

"How far did you read?"

"Seven chapters."

"Oh, boy."

"So what you wrote about in the book, I *was* wondering—"

"Here it comes."

"Here what comes?"

"*Is it autobiographical.*"

He handed her the bread as he sat down. "Is it?"

With her eyes down, she shook her head as she tore off a piece of bread and handed the basket back to him. "That's the three point five million dollar question."

"What do you mean?"

"That's the question I hear most often, the question that ended my marriage. Although my husband wasn't wild about the genre initially, once it was successful, he professed to being proud of me. That's a *professor* for you. Then he couldn't handle all the questions and innuendo from his friends and colleagues. Are we swingers? Do we have three-ways? You know, if I wrote about zombies or vampires, no one would ask if I were a revenant—the living dead."

"True enough." He chuckled. "But I really didn't think that you were into three-ways."

"No? Why not?" she asked, once again able to face him, the candlelight flickering on her skin and reflecting in her eyes.

"For one thing, you said yourself that, based on the sales, a lot of women must have ménage *fantasies*."

"That was the other thing Martin—that's my husband…my *ex*-husband—suspected: that I wanted to have a *ménage à trois*. Then he would accuse me of wanting to bring one man or another, someone we knew or he worked with or even saw in a restaurant, into bed with us. 'What about him? How about so-and-so? Do you want him?' His paranoia exhausted me, always having to defend myself for thoughts I didn't even have."

"So you don't have fantasies like that?"

Her cheeks flamed. "Not like that, with a third person, but my fantasies are my own. I know it's what I write about, but this is getting a little personal. I'm sure you have sexual fantasies."

"Of course. In fact, several just this evening. But never a three-way. Some things I refuse to share." While she struggled with a response, he scraped his chair against the floor as he stood to serve the lasagna, her wide eyes following him into the kitchen. "Would you like me to fix your plate?"

"Please."

"That's kind of chickenshit, if you don't mind my saying, that your ex reacted like that."

She sniffed with amusement. "No, I don't mind."

"He sounds pretty weak. A husband should be the one person a wife can rely on. He's supposed to protect her, stand by her."

With a quick lift of her eyebrows, she said, "Now *that's* a fantasy."

"It doesn't have to be. You said he's a professor?"

"Adjunct at The King's College. English lit."

"That's no excuse. He should have stood up for

you. Maybe he's just intimidated by your success."

"The irony of it is that he had barely walked out the door when he told me he's dating one of his former students. So here he was accusing me of lusting after other men when he's the one with someone already waiting in the wings."

Setting their plates down, he returned to his seat. "That's typical, accusing someone of something he's guilty of himself. Since he's doing it, it makes him suspicious. Do you think they were seeing each other while you were still together?"

"If so, they'd have to be extremely careful. I might have been naïve, but King's is an extremely conservative Christian college, Campus Crusade for Christ and all that. Faculty even have to sign a statement of faith. I think one of their presidents had to resign because he got engaged before his divorce was final. On the other hand, it certainly would explain all of those late nights Martin spent in his office. I really should have been suspicious since that's how he and I got together."

"You were one of his students at King's, too?

"This was at St. John's. I was a T.A. in the English department, and he was on the faculty there when we met, but I was never one of his students; however, we did spend plenty of time in his office alone together."

"So same M.O." Topping off their wine glasses, he said, "In any case, no, I wasn't going to ask you if that was autobiographical; but out of curiosity, how did you end up writing ménage books if, you know, that's not your thing?"

"For years, I wrote sweet romances—

contemporary, romantic suspense, whatever—and couldn't make a profit. Every penny I made in royalties, I just turned around and invested on promotions. Then I got to be friends with another author, Jack Clifford. You know, I'm staying in his parents' cabin."

"Oh, William Fitzpatrick."

"It's Patrick Fitzwilliam." Then she caught the gleam in his eye and gave him a light shove. "And you know it! He writes male/male paranormal romances and does quite well. He said that if I really wanted to make money, I should write MMMFMM erotic romances."

"MMMF?"

"Male male male female..." she said then returned to her food and wine.

"Jesus, how many males is that? Sounds like a sausagefes—sounds kind of crowded."

"I couldn't go from writing sweet romances to writing orgies. So I came up with an idea for a two-part ménage story. Then the first one went through the roof, and the publisher signed me to a three-book deal. Unfortunately, I have no idea what the third novel should be about, and the deadline is only a few weeks away."

"And that's why you came up here, to get away from everything and write? I hope I'm not keeping you from your work."

"I still have to eat. Besides, did you see the film *The Shining*? 'All work and no play…' OK, so if you weren't going to ask me if it's autobiographical, then what was your question?"

Sam finished chewing, swallowed, blotted his mouth with his napkin, drank some wine, then caught her in his stare. "Why is it that the girl in the book— Em—this strong, confident, career-oriented, successful woman, wants to be dominated? Why does she like to be tied up?"

Gillian flushed, eyes downcast, then took a sip of wine. "This lasagna really is good."

"I promise, next time I really will cook for you, but it's more likely to be steak and potatoes. Unless you'd like me to be a gentleman and take you out to dinner."

"You don't have to do that. Steak and potatoes is fine."

He leaned closer to her, bracing himself on the back of her chair with his arm resting along her shoulder. "Is that because going to a restaurant would make it a real date, or you don't want me to be a gentleman?"

They both stopped eating, drinking, breathing through several restless heartbeats, the tension taut between them.

After another sip of wine, she met his stare again and licked her lips, drawing his gaze to her mouth for just a moment before the magnetic force returned it to her eyes.

"Maybe I just like steak," she said on a soft breath.

"You still haven't answered my question."

"What question is that?"

"Why does Em like to be tied up?"

"Does that mean you're not going to finish?"

The hand on the back of her chair caressed the nape of her neck then brushed down her hair. He angled his face close enough that they shared the same Chiantiimbrued breath. "I always finish what I've started."

"Then you'll just need to keep going a little further to find out."

"I'll go as far as you let me."

Shaking off the raw current sizzling through her, she said, "I must have had too much wine. Is this still about my novel?"

"Do you want it to be?"

She bit her bottom lip as she smiled. "Can I decide later?"

He lifted his hand and ran his fingertips along her hairline, against her temple, over her ear, then down her neck before twisting a lock of hair around his forefinger. As he did so, her lips parted and her eyelids fluttered down. She opened them, and he fixed her in his piercing stare. "Of course," he said.

A lengthy, nervous breath escaped her pursed lips. "I…I'm sorry. I don't remember how to do this."

"I think you're doing all right."

"Um, we should probably eat before our food gets cold."

He let her hair slip through his fingers as he sat back with a grin. "That's another reason I knew it wasn't autobiographical."

"What's that?"

"You might flirt and talk a big game, but then you always wind up blushing."

"What? I, uh…No, I don't."

"You do. That's a compliment. It's quite fetching."

She forced her eyes away from his and drank from her glass. "I think that's enough about me," she said. "How long have you been police chief?"

"Going on seven years now."

"Before that?"

"I got my degree in criminal justice at Seattle U., and after graduation, I stayed in Washington State. Eventually, I became a detective with the Seattle Police Department."

"From detective in a major city to police chief in a small town? That's quite a career move."

"Well, my folks are from Upstate, and they were getting older. When my mom got sick, I wanted to move out here."

"You have brothers, sisters?"

"No, only child."

"So the responsibility fell to you. Your parents are still up here?"

"They've both passed now."

"Oh. I'm so sorry."

"It's been a few years. Like I said, I made my peace with my dad before he died."

"Did your wife come with you from Seattle?"

"She tried but it didn't take. Even before then, I think she'd stopped liking me very much. I guess I'd hoped a change in venue might, you know, bring us back together, but it drove us further apart. She's all about being self-sufficient, independent."

"Nothing wrong with that."

"Of course not, but she wanted autonomy, and I'm the kind of man who likes to be needed."

"Is that why you chose to go into law enforcement? Saving damsels in distress?"

He smiled with a soft laugh as he glanced at her. "Maybe."

"Any children?"

"A daughter. Fourteen." He pulled out his wallet and showed her a school portrait.

She set down her fork to take the photo then handed it back to him. "Pretty."

"She lives in Seattle with her mother. I don't see her often. How about you? Kids?"

"Yes. Two daughters from my first marriage."

"Two ex-husbands?" She nodded. "Do the girls live with you or with their father?"

"Iiiiiiiiiii'd rather not say."

"Oh." He blinked in confusion several times. "All right. Should I open that other bottle of wine?" He stood and headed toward the kitchen.

"I, uh, I don't know. I'm already a little fuzzy-headed."

"Well, it's not like you're driving." He twisted the cork out and brought the bottle to the table.

"But I am alone in a cabin in the middle of nowhere with a strange man."

"I'm not so strange once you get to know me."

"I haven't even seen your real home. You could have a wife or girlfriend or a pit with some girl putting on lotion from a basket."

He laughed. "You can check it out any time you like, but then you can never leave," he said with an ominous tone, and she chuckled. "It's not much to see. I'm sure nothing compared to your place."

"In Manhattan? Oh, it's actually exactly like this."

"Really?"

"Mmmhmm."

"A cabin in the woods in the Flatiron District."

"Hey! How did you know I lived in Flatiron?"

"The detective who called said they were alerting the *staff* at your building. Must be quite a cabin. How do I know you don't have some poor man chained up in your BDSM dungeon next to your catsuit and flogger?"

"But you're the one with the handcuffs."

"Well, I *am* the police chief." He splashed more wine into her empty glass. "Don't worry. I promise not to use them until you want me to."

Her eyes glimmered in the candlelight as she brought the glass to her lips.

He told her more about himself and his past as they ate and drank wine, and then she spoke of her childhood in Connecticut as she helped him with the dishes, over his protests. They finished the wine on the couch in front of the wood burning stove in his living room, talking, with smiles and laughter and the occasional casual touch, reacting with awe-stricken delight when discovering anything they found they had in common.

Then, the lasagna, the dishes, and the wine were done, leaving them alone in the room rife with heady anticipation.

"I think I better get going," she said.

"What about the s'mores?"

"I don't think I can handle any s'more tonight." She came to her feet, and he followed. "Save the s'mores for next time?"

"I like the way that sounds."

"What's that?"

"That you want there to be a 'next time.' I'll hold

on to your marshmallows as collateral. If you insist on leaving now, I'll drive you home."

"You don't have to drive me to the cabin. I've walked through Harlem at two a.m."

"Then I'll walk with you." He slid her heavy sweater onto her arms and shoulders, lifting her hair over the collar, his fingers lingering on the nape of her neck. "What kind of gentleman would I be if I didn't walk you home?"

She glanced up at him over her shoulder. "So you are a *gentleman* after all?"

He gazed down at her as he massaged her neck. "Can I decide later?" Her eyes widened, and he smiled. "Regardless, I am an officer of the law. I have a sworn duty to protect and defend."

"From owls and hawks?"

"And maybe a possum. C'mon, you're not going without me."

They walked along the lake, the crescent moon reflected in its waters, speaking of nothing and everything. At some point, either by accident or on purpose, their hands bumped together, and he took hers and held it as they continued down the shoreline accompanied by an orchestra of wildlife. He shone his flashlight at a hooting owl and tried to catch the eyes of a deer or a coyote on the other side of the lake.

At one point, a cry echoed out in the night, and she started and clutched his bicep. "Oh, my god! What was that?"

He suppressed his chuckle as he tilted his head toward hers. "It's just a fox."

She relaxed against him. "It sounds like a woman

screaming."

"Yeah, we locals do that on purpose to get pretty girls from the city to hold onto them." She giggled, and he grinned. "No, it's true! We have those foxes specially trained!"

"Foxes for foxes, eh?"

They arrived at her cabin, and she turned around to face him. "Well, this is the street where I live."

"So what did you decide?" he asked. "Was this a date?"

The corners of her lips rose, exposing her teeth in the glint of the moon. "I think so. Yes."

"Good. Then I can do this." Taylor caught her off guard, pulling her tight against him as his mouth overtook hers.

She did not resist, though. She raised her hands to rest upon his shoulders and, closing her eyes, opened her mouth to submit, accepting his tongue against her own, as a ribbon of heat rippled through them both. They kissed like this, lips and teeth clashing, tongues entangled, mouths consuming, for several minutes before she withdrew, chest heaving and out of breath, and dropped her head.

"You know," she said, "I'm not the heroine from my novels. I'm not even the person I pretend to be as P.G. Tate."

"I know." He lifted her chin and met her eyes in the dim moonlight, his own breathing labored.

"I don't go to bed with someone on the first date."

He grazed his fingers down her cheek. "I'm glad for that."

Then he covered her mouth with his again, sinking

his tongue in deep, his hands on her upper arms with a grip so firm, holding her tight against his chest, it must surely leave a mark.

When he finally broke the blistering kiss, he heaved out an extended audible breath. "Whew." Gazing into her eyes, he drew a finger down her cheek. "I'll see you tomorrow. Steak?"

She nodded, then he watched her walk into her cabin and close the door. She peered out the window as he continued to stare at the cabin for a while before turning and strutting back up the lake.

Everything they did, every moment they shared, every word, every thought, every touch, every kiss, Gillian captured on paper. She documented each look and sigh as if she were a teenager writing in a diary, rather than releasing anything so thrilling, exciting, sensual to the inconstancy of memory.

Chapter 6

Gillian had her phone on as she drove, glancing at it occasionally to check the reception, but it continued to read "No Service" for over three miles until she got into the middle of town. With the first bar, the intonations of musical notes had her grabbing it and parking in the first spot she found. Two texts and three voicemails, all from Sunday evening. She read the texts first, both from Jack.

> OMG! You wont believe who was just here looking for you COPS!!! Call me! They wouldnt tell me why but had to tell them where UR. WTF???

Immediately followed by:

> What have you been doing???
> You whore!

She laughed then listened to her voicemail. First a sniffling Sarah:

"Hi Gillian. I got your voicemail so you probably won't get this for a while, but someone broke into my house and stole my laptop and iPad. You're probably going to hear from the police because...well, call me when you can."

Second, from Jack:

"Oh my god! What the fuck is going on? The police were just here! I bet you never listen to voicemail. I'll text you."

Third voicemail:

"Mrs. Tate, this is Detective Ed Bennet with NYPD out of Brooklyn. Your agent—Sarah Falgert—her home office was burglarized and her laptop stolen. It contained personal information about you. We don't know if the break-in is related to the threatening letters you've received, but I have informed the personnel at your building. Also, I obtained your location from Jack Clifford, so I'll be sending the local authorities to check on you. If you have any questions or information, call me at 718-439...."

Gillian called each of her daughters first, checking in without telling them about the threats. She had texted them her plans to go Upstate but just left it at needing isolation to finish her novel. She gave them

Sam Taylor's name and number in case of an emergency but didn't mention he was the police chief.

Next she called Jack, and it rolled to voicemail. "Hi, Jack. Do you listen to *your* voice mail? For your information, I did not do anything. Someone broke into Sarah's house and they thought it might be related to the hate mail I've been getting. Love the cabin, by the way. Lake Kiwassa is amazing, the way the trees reflect in it, almost like a mirror. And why didn't you tell me about the police chief? He is..." As her eyes roamed the ceiling of the car as if in search of an adjective, her face flushed and she released a long exhalation. "Well, I'm sure you know. I'll call you next time I'm in town."

Then she texted him:

Listen to your vmail ;)

When she clicked to call Sarah, her agent came on with the first ring. "Gillian, thank god you're OK."

"Me! How are you?"

"So the police talked to you? I'm better, now. It was a mess to clean up, and I just got a new laptop. Fortunately, I had everything backed up in the clouds, so I didn't lose much. But whoever did it got the phone numbers and addresses of all my clients."

"Nothing about the girls, right?"

"No, I swear it. Everything just as P.G. Tate. Never any association with your daughters, not even their last name, ever.

"Thanks, Sarah."

"Gillian, I am so, so sorry."

"Don't worry about it. It wasn't your fault. Plus, don't they need your password to get in anyway?"

"I have no idea. There must be some way around that, like one of those F keys. The police didn't seem to think that would stop them."

"Can't you use 'Find my iPad' or whatever?"

"Didn't work. I guess it has to be turned on. Speaking of being turned on, how's the new book coming?"

"I, uh. I haven't quite started."

"What!"

"I've still been tired from all this traveling. But," she bit her bottom lip as the corners of her mouth lifted her cheeks. "I have found some inspiration. I met someone."

"You're kidding. I thought you were in the middle of nowhere."

"Actually, believe it or not, it's thanks to those psychos, or whoever robbed your place. It's the police chief that came to tell me about your break-in."

"Only you, Gillian. You can't find a date in a city of two million people then fall in love with the first person you meet Upstate."

"I'm not in love. We just met! But, whew." She dropped her head back against the car seat and closed her eyes.

"Come on, tell me. What's he like?"

"Tall, strong, funny, smart, a good dancer, an amazing kisser."

"You already kissed him? OK, you're a goner."

"Stop that! It's just, well…I enjoy being with him. I enjoy thinking about him when I'm not with him. I just…really like him."

"What are you going to do with your Manhattan penthouse when you move to the Adirondacks?"

She lurched forward and opened her eyes with a frown. "I hadn't thought of that. In any case, *we just met*. You're getting way ahead of the game. It's a moot point. He hasn't even seen me undressed. I'm sure once he gets to know me better, he'll lose interest."

"Uh-huh. You've been out of the game too long if that's what you think. Is he age-appropriate?"

"What's that supposed to mean? Why can't a woman over forty date a younger man without being labeled a predatory animal?"

"I know you. Younger is definitely not your type."

She released a sigh rippled with aggravation. "OK, yes. I think mid-forties. And oh, so my type."

"So nothing like your ex-husbands."

Gillian giggled. "Exactly."

"I hope you get used to those winters up there."

"Shut up! There's nothing wrong with kissing, is there?"

"Just as long as you stop there."

Gillian's cell phone buzzed in her ear and she glanced at the screen. "Shit. I didn't charge my cell phone enough, and it's about to die. You have twenty percent to tell me everything I need to know."

"OK, well your editor called wanting an update on your progress—no surprise there…."

Before ending the call, Sarah said, "Gillian, there was one more thing. Another message from the Sword of the Archangel."

"Lovely. What is it this time? I'm making people wear cotton polyester blends?"

"No, but it is another biblical passage. It has Jacob in a tizzy again with his same spiel about being your agent."

"Let's hear it." Sarah read it to her, and Gillian rubbed her eyes with her thumb and finger. "OK, just give it to that detective. I don't even want to think about those wackos. Thanks, Sarah. My phone's almost dead. I'll call you in a few days."

"Fuck!" Gillian said when she saw the police lights behind her as she drove away from town, her heart rate accelerating, a response ingrained in the collective unconscious. She pulled over and turned off the engine but then smiled at the image in the rearview mirror, the Chief's strong, tall form in his uniform, no hat or sunglasses, walking toward her from his patrol car.

When he got to her door, she rolled down the window. "Is that a pistol in your holster, or are you just glad to see me?"

Resting his arms on the roof of her car, he leaned toward the window with a grin, meeting her eyes. "Ma'am."

"Is there a problem, Officer?"

"Do you know how fast you were going?" he asked, playing along.

"How fast do you want me to be?"

He snickered and glanced over his shoulder at his patrol car before looking back at her. "Do you talk to all men like that? All this sexual innuendo?"

"I told you I'm out of practice. Maybe you just bring it out in me."

"I'd like to believe that."

"Well, this *is* out of one of my fantasies."

"What is?"

"Being pulled over by a good-looking cop and getting frisked, then...doing whatever's necessary to get myself out of a ticket."

He swallowed then leaned through her window and spoke against her ear. "If it weren't the middle of the day, and if there weren't a dash-cam on that patrol car, I'd have you step out of your vehicle, assume the position, and spread your legs." He stepped back as a heated flush overwhelmed her face.

"So." She choked on the word through her nerves then cleared her throat before speaking again, catching a glimpse of his smug smile. "So, Officer, are you stopping me on official police business?"

"I do enjoy making you blush. But no, I just saw you driving in town. You could have stopped by the police station."

"I wouldn't want to bother you at work. I just came down to call Sarah, see if she's doing OK and tell her how sorry I am. I would have done it yesterday if I hadn't slept all day."

"How is she doing? Did they catch the perp?"

"No, but she's doing better than I would be. There was another message from the Archangel group, though, so now her husband is pressuring her to stop representing me. Again."

"Why? What was the message?"

She faced forward toward the windshield but with her eyes on the steering wheel. "Uh, just more of the same, really. I didn't write it down."

When she said nothing more nor even turned back to him, he changed the subject. "We hadn't said a time for tonight, and of course I can't call you. I've been thinking of getting you a two-way."

She looked back up at him with a grin. "As opposed to a three-way?"

"Clever. A two-way radio. Can I see your mobile phone?"

"Sure." She handed it to him.

No Service.

"Yeah, you'll never get any reception with this provider outside of town." Then he thumbed through the apps and frowned. "What's this text message? 'What have you been doing, you whore?'"

"Nosey!" She grabbed the phone from him. "That's just my friend Jack."

"That sounds pretty hostile. Are you sure he's not responsible for the messages? You know, usually the perp is someone acquainted with the victim."

Rolling her eyes up to him with amusement, she said, "Definitely not Jack. He was just being silly. Trust me."

"All right, if you say so. How 'bout I pick you up at six-thirty?"

"You don't have to pick me up."

"Yes, I do. Otherwise, you'll just walk again." He straightened up and knocked on the roof of her car. "OK, I'll let you off with a warning this time, but if I catch you again, you'll get what's coming to you."

She watched in her side-view mirror as he sauntered away.

Armed for war, the Sword of Michael the Archangel had the power, the weapon of knowledge. Guided by the information obtained from Sarah's office, the mighty Sword would wield its justice, casting the fornicators, the sodomites, and she—who misleads the servants of the Lord into committing acts of immorality—onto a bed of suffering.

The Sword had been led astray, seduced into the ways of sexual immorality, by the one who debauches others with her words, a Jezebel who uses her witchcraft and whoredom, lauded and aggrandized as a prophetess. The only path to save itself for the glory of God is for the Sword to repent and renounce her ways, strike her down and make those who commit sin with her suffer intensely.

The Lord God delivered the sodomite unto the Avenging Angel through that sinner's blasphemy—the glorification of his sexual immorality through the blatant unholy mockery of the Word of God in his public appeal, calling on others to join him in his den of iniquity.

On Facebook, Patrick Fitzwilliam had posted his status update:

> Going to The Metro in the
> Village for drinks and dancing
> tonight – who's with me?

Chapter 7

"So, I, uh…finished your book," Sam said after dinner as he poured them each another glass of wine.

"Wow, you're a fast reader." Gillian accepted the glass from him as he sat down beside her on the couch in front of the wood burning stove.

"I guess it depends on what I'm reading."

"I'm afraid to ask what you thought."

"For one thing, there's something so authentic about the character of Em."

"Authentic?"

"I can see traces of you in her."

"She's nothing like me!"

"Well, on the surface, but there's an underlying vulnerability. She needs something else, something more…" She didn't respond aside from drinking her wine, and he didn't press her. "And I knew it wasn't going to end well for Harry."

"Don't worry about Harry. He gets his 'happily ever after' in the sequel. All my stories have a happily ever after."

"But he's bisexual, right? So does he end up with a man or a woman?"

"A man. The second novel focuses on the male/male relationship, which is why all the homophobes came out of the woodwork and started harassing me."

"Gillian, I gotta say…your sex scenes—"

"Oh, no." She covered her eyes with her hand.

"They are quite…intense. And explicit."

She inhaled deeply and released a long, quavering breath. "I know."

Setting his wine down, he grasped her wrist to pull her hand away from her face. "What's wrong? Why are you turning red?"

"It's just…embarrassing to talk about it as myself and not P.G. Tate." She took a sip of her wine before placing her glass next to his and returning her eyes to him. "Especially with a man."

"We don't have to talk about it. As explicit as the sex scenes are, I was just curious about how you wrote the second novel."

"What do you mean?"

"In *Lying in Petals*, even though it was a ménage, both men only…"

"Only what?"

"Sorry, it's just that in your book, you use rather frank language about sex. Since we've only known each other a few days, I don't want to be presumptuous and think you like to use those sexual terms in real life if it's just for your writing."

She averted her eyes and hid her shy smile by taking a sip of wine. "So you mean in *Petals*, it was just straight sex, male/female."

"Hmm…all right. We'll leave that other topic alone

for now. So, yes, both men have sex just with Em, not with each other. Now assuming that you are not now nor have ever been a gay man—and god, I hope that assumption is correct—how did you write the male/male sex scenes in the sequel?"

She laughed. "Yes, it's true, not having ever been a gay man was a challenge. I kept getting stuck there. I finally just decided to write the story like any other romance novel and come back and add the sex scenes later. I still had to do quite a bit of research on gay sex though."

Taylor almost blew out the wine he had just swallowed. "Research?"

"Well, first I interviewed Jack and a couple of my other gay friends, and they went into all the graphic details, some of which were *not* romantic at all."

"To be honest, I don't find any of it romantic."

"Which is why I said you probably wouldn't like the second novel. But no matter how much I talked to them about it, I just couldn't picture it in my head; and I have to be able to 'see' something before I can write about it."

"I'm getting worried where you're going with this."

"Well, I finally broke down and watched my first porn movie—a gay porno."

He threw his head back and laughed then shook his head. "I am so relieved you said that."

"Why? What did you think I was going to say?"

"It doesn't matter. So how did you get this gay porn movie? Borrow it from your friend Jack?"

"Actually, that never occurred to me. I knew that they had all those so-called 'adult' channels on pay-per-view, and I'm really blocked with my writing. Then I thought, 'Huh. I wonder if they have any gay porn on those channels.' Sure enough..."

He drew his brows together as he continued to watch her. "And this surprised you?"

"Oh, hush. Like how would I know? Then I find one that's a gay porn version of that old Guy Ritchie film *Lock, Stock, and Two Smoking Barrels*. I thought this was perfect because one of my characters is British so maybe I could pick up some British gay slang, you know?"

"Well, of course. That's only logical."

She slapped his arm playfully. "Are you making fun of me?"

"Who, me? Tease you?" He brought her hand to his grinning lips and kissed her fingers. "Please continue, my sweet. Did this help you with your writing?

"I think so, but I did have a few complications."

"What kind of complications? Or dare I ask?"

"The entire time I'm watching it, I'm taking meticulous notes; but most of the, uh, actors have thick British dialects. So I kept pausing and backing up and tried to hear what they were saying, so I had the volume up pretty loud. My husband and I were living in our old apartment with neighbors on either side. The, um, sounds in the sex scenes are rather distinct, so there is no way in hell the neighbors didn't know I was watching porn."

Gillian started chuckling as she continued the story, and Taylor joined her as he listened.

"Now, I have to preface this next part by admitting that both my daughters are in their twenties, but let's just leave it at that for now."

"Uh, oh. How are your daughters involved?"

"I'm watching this on a Saturday afternoon, right? Then my younger daughter called and asked what I was doing, and I said, 'I'm watching gay porn. Want to come over and watch it with me?' She said, 'No, thanks. I just got out of the gym, so I'm going home to shower. I'm all nasty and sweaty.' Then we chat a few more minutes about whatever. Did not even ask why I was watching gay porn."

"You're kidding," he said through his laughter.

She shook her head. "Nope. Later, that's what I said. 'You know, you didn't even ask why I was watching gay porn,' and she said, 'I figured you were just doing research on a new book.'"

"Smart girl. More wine?"

"I, uh…I don't know. I'm already kind of tipsy."

"That's OK. I'm driving you home." He refilled her glass and handed it to her. "And what happened with the movie?"

"One last thing about my daughter. So my *other* daughter called and I related that story to her, and she said, 'You know, Mom, she didn't dismiss your invitation out of hand—just that she couldn't come over *right then*. The implication being that in other circumstances she may have been down with watching gay porn.'"

"That's hysterical."

"I know, right?"

"Your daughters sound great. So is that why you didn't want to say where they lived? Because they're on their own?"

"Yes! Because it makes me sound so old."

"If you have adult daughters, I'd guess they are either your step-daughters or you had them when you were ten."

"The older they get, the younger I become when I had them! Actually, I'm just a walking cliché. I got pregnant losing my virginity on the night of my senior prom."

"I bet that caused some friction with your parents."

"You have no idea. But back to this 'movie.'"

"Oh, god, there's more?"

"Oh, yeah. I had a major dilemma. It was supposed to be an hour and twenty-five minutes long, but after fifty-five minutes, it just stopped. I can't exactly call the cable company and complain, hey, I was watching this gay porn flick and it stopped in the middle. At this point, I really did have enough notes for my research. In fact, I had started fast-forwarding through the sex scenes because they were getting kind of redundant, and I really started worrying about these guys getting TMJ." Taylor choked on his wine as he barked out a laugh, and she slapped him on the back. "Are you OK?" He nodded even as he shook his head, his eyes watering. "All right, well, the thing is, it did have some semblance of a plot, and now I'm never going to find out what happens to Sergio's money!"

"Christ, you're killing me."

"So I call my daughter back and tell her about it stopping in the middle, and she says to call the cable company and complain, that they won't know I'm watching porn. I said, 'Dana, the movie is called *Lock, Stock, and British Cocks*. I think they'll figure it out!'"

"Jesus, that's unbelievable," he said, shaking his head as their laughter receded

"I swear, it's all true."

"It's too unbelievable *not* to be true!" They both drank from their wine, which assisted their efforts to subdue their laughter. "But that does bring me back to the other topic."

"Which is?"

"The language you use in your novels, like the name of the movie: Is that just in your writing?"

"I don't know what you mean." Her eyes followed her hand as she set her glass down and remained there.

"Yes, you do. Do you only use 'cock' in your books?"

"Why? Does profanity offend you? I get that a lot."

"Quite the opposite." He moved closer to her and placed his hand on her neck, turning her head to face him. "But is that you or just *P.G.* Tate? Do you like it when someone tells you they want to *fuck* you?"

Scarlet bloomed in her cheeks. "No one has ever said that to me before?"

"Not even your husband—or husband*s*?"

She shook her head.

Taylor rubbed her jaw with his thumb as he penetrated her with his gaze. "What if I say I want to *fuck* you?"

Her pulse throbbed erratically against his palm, and her breath caught in her throat. "I'd say I'm not ready. It's too soon."

"That's fine. I'd never pressure you." He pulled her near enough to him that his breath swept across her lips. "But does it bother you if I say I want to fuck you?"

"No."

Her eyes closed and her shallow breaths accelerated as he laid a path of kisses from the corner of her mouth across her cheek to her ear. "Do you like me to say I want to fuck you?"

She leaned her head back, and he blazed a trail of fire on her neck, the blood racing in her veins beating against his lips.

"Yes."

"Why?"

On a low breath she said, "Because I want you to fuck me."

"Good. I'm pleased to hear you say that."

"Just…not yet. Like you said, we've only known each other a few days."

He lifted his face to meet her eyes again, sliding his arms around her. "I know." Then he crushed her mouth with his, capturing her moan and claiming it as his own. His tongue plunged into her welcoming mouth as she circled her arms around his neck, deepening the kiss. She combed her fingers through his hair and rolled her tongue around his as a swirl of heat surrounded them.

When he raised his face, the wrinkle that formed between her brows tugged at the corners of his mouth. He stretched past her and turned off the lamp on the end table, leaving them with only the dim light shining in from the kitchen and the flickering flames of the burning wood in the stove.

"Why did you do that?"

"Because I don't want the light to be in your eyes,"

he said, rearranging the throw pillows and settling her back upon them, "when you lie down." She nudged off her shoes as he lifted her legs onto the sofa then leaned over her. With his weight on his forearms on either side of her head, he teased her lips apart with his tongue then explored her mouth with a thoroughness that left them both breathless.

When he came up for air, he said, "I love these dresses you wear."

"They hide a multitude of flaws."

"Don't ever say anything like that again. You are the sexiest woman I have ever seen." His lips followed his fingers along the buttons on the front of her dress, releasing each one slowly and placing a kiss on the newly-exposed skin down her chest and between her breasts.

"Wait," she said on a rush of breath, grasping his shoulders. He pushed himself up on one arm and gazed down into her glittering eyes. "I-I said it was too soon."

Leaving one hand against her pounding heart, he traced her forehead and cheek with the fingers of the other, his ragged breath caressing her face. "Gillian, you can trust me. I promise, as badly as I want to, I will not fuck you tonight."

"Then what are you doing?"

"As much as you'll let me." He smiled and slipped his hand under the lace covering her breast and circled her nipple with his fingertips, provoking a gasp. "We're not kids, Gillian. This isn't prom night. I admit I want to put my hands all over your body, but we'll stop whenever you want. Just tell me. Do you only want to kiss?"

"I…" Her eyelids slid halfway down as her nipple hardened under his playful attention. "I love the way you kiss. It's been so long since anyone kissed me."

"It's been a long time for me, too, and I'm not finished by a long shot." As if to prove the veracity of his words, he reclaimed her lips, tasting the pleasures of her mouth and drawing the passion from within her along with her breath. "Should I stop there?" He tweaked her nipple. "Or shall I continue?"

"Yes."

He kissed her again. "Yes, stop, or yes, continue?"

"Oh, yes, please continue."

A soft laugh escaped with his heavy breath, and he massaged her breast. "Do you have any other hard limits?"

Her eyes flared with recognition of the words from her own novel. "Hard limits?"

"I already promised not to fuck you tonight. Anything else that's a definite no?"

She bit her bottom lip, staring up at him in the flickering light, her heartbeats rapid and breathing labored under the hand on her breast. "Uh-oral."

"Well, that's a shame, but OK. Now slide down here and let me make love to you." He withdrew his fingers from the opening in her dress then maneuvered her farther down the couch, stretching her arms over her head and clasping her wrists in one hand as he bent over her. He kissed her mouth with such heat until she melted under him and purred. "There, that's much better. Now where was I?"

His hand returned to fondle her breast while he

kissed her lips, her jaw, her neck, her chest. He pushed the lace down to expose her nipple then licked it into a hard peak. He sucked it into his mouth, causing her to groan and his cock to throb in his jeans.

Taylor had yet to release her wrists when he returned to the plunder of her mouth, while his other hand drew her dress up until its hem rose above her knees. Her lips quivered against his as he caressed the inside of her lush, creamy thigh up to the silk between her legs. He lifted his head only enough to see her swollen mouth and sleepy eyes. "I love your dresses, but I can't say I approve of these." He watched her face as his fingers wandered up to the lace waistband and slipped under the silk. Lust flashed in her eyes with her serrated breath when he touched her clit. He rolled his fingers around it then slid them down her slit, barely dipping inside of her, eliciting a jagged inhalation. "I noticed you didn't use any slang for *this*." He swirled his fingers in her hot core.

"I...I haven't found one that's not used as an insulting epithet." Her quiet words floated out on air. "I hate them all; they're so course and..." She lost her voice when his touch ventured deeper.

"God, you are so wet," he said, his words soft with his shallow breathing. "You *do* want me to fuck you, don't you?" Her dilated eyes wide and her breath coming in rapid huffs, she twisted her wrists in his grasp, but he tightened his hold. "Shhh, it's OK. Relax. Trust. Remember? I don't mean now, tonight. I'm just looking forward to the day I do. I like knowing how aroused I can make you."

"Are you sure you haven't been plying me with

alcohol to take advantage of me?"

"That's exactly what I've been doing." As he ran his fingertips in a steady pattern up and around her clit then down again, slipping inside of her with each pass, she relaxed and groaned. "Are you all right now? Do you want me to stop?"

"Please, no, don't stop," she said, her voice raspy.

"You never told me why Em likes to be tied up."

When the pleasure of his touch did not force her eyes closed, she kept gazing up at him. "Mer—" The word scattered on her trembling breath. "Merintho…philia."

"You remember, I finished your book. I know why she wants to be tied up. She needs to give up control. I think that's part of you—you're the same way. You want a man who frees you by taking control. Am I right?"

She forced her reply out on soft breaths. "Yes."

"Releasing you of all the pressure, all the worries."

"Yes."

He lay against her, kissing her neck as he thrust his fingers deeper inside of her. "Freeing you of inhibitions. Freeing your mind, just to be, to be right here with me…just to feel."

Her eyes closed as she stretched her neck back toward where he held her wrists, allowing him greater access. "Yes," she said on a soft groan.

He pressed his lips to hers, sharing a kiss ripe with promise and demand, sending shockwaves of sensation through them both as the rest of the world fell away, leaving just a man and a woman in desperate need of one another.

She whined when he sat up, releasing her mouth and her wrists and withdrawing his hand from between her legs. "I have to stop a second," he said, then brought his wine glass to his lips with an unsteady hand. "Whew." He ran his fingers through his hair then glanced back to where she lay with a slight smile aimed at him.

She raised herself up part way, her head braced on one hand with her elbow on the couch. "Do you want me to go?" she asked, a glint in her eyes.

He set his glass down then turned to her and shook his head, grinning back at her with fire in his eyes. "No. I want you to come." Blood rose in her cheeks as his hands traveled up the skirt of her dress. "But these *do* have to go—totally unnecessary," he said, rolling the lingerie down her legs and off her feet.

"Uhh…I don't think…"

"Good, then don't." He pulled her into his arms, pushed her back against the pillows, and sought her mouth again. She wrapped her arms around his neck, but as they kissed, she began to giggle. He rested his forehead on hers, meeting her twinkling eyes. "Not exactly the response I was going for. You find something amusing, sweetheart?"

She shrugged against the cushions. "I, uh, I don't know. Maybe I shouldn't say this, but I really enjoy being with you."

"Why shouldn't you say it? I think it's pretty clear how much I enjoy being with you."

"I guess I laughed because I'm having fun."

"Good. Me, too."

"It's been a long time."

He kissed her with a tenderness that sent shivers rippling through her. "Me, too," he said.

Held in this embrace, staring into each other's eyes, their smiles faded. Their hearts pounded in rapid synchronicity, trepidation from something other than desire. He raised his hand to her face and caressed her cheek with his fingertips, this gentle act setting their pulses racing.

After too many moments had passed listening to their own breaths, Taylor broke the silence and the spell. "Would you like—" He stopped himself and instead said, "I'm going to handcuff you."

Her gaze dropped, thoughts rushing through her mind evident in her features. Then she met his questioning eyes. "Where?" she asked.

"Around your wrists, of course." The previous lightness returned to his tone.

She laughed and shoved his arm. "You know what I mean. Do you want to handcuff me *to* something?"

"Uh, no. Just behind your back. You'll stand up."

"You've done this before?"

"No. Never. I mean, yes, when I've arrested someone, but never like this. Not for the reasons I want to cuff you."

"Have you been planning this?"

"Not planning, but I admit I have been thinking about it since you mentioned it last night."

After a few beats of her heart, she said, "OK. Yes."

He stood then helped her to her feet and handed her her wine. "Stay here. I'll be right back." When he walked away toward his bedroom, she drank down the contents of her glass in one swallow. He returned with the cuffs and stood at the end of the couch. "Come here."

She stepped over to him, and he turned her around, pulling one hand behind her back. "You do have the keys, right?"

"Shhh." He snapped the cuff around her wrist with a clink. "Other hand." She stuck her arm behind her back, the trembling that had taken over her body flowing down through her fingertips. He closed the other ring around her wrist, binding her hands together, which thrust her breasts forward. "Nervous?" he said against her ear.

Her chest rising and falling with quick, uneven breaths, she couldn't deny it and said nothing.

He walked around to face her and coiled his fingers in her hair, tugging on it to tilt her head back. "OK?" he asked, his voice low and his eyes meeting hers. She nodded as much as his grip would allow. He kissed her with such hunger, his mouth raging for satiation, he stole her breath away. When he finally drew back, they were both red and panting. He pulled the sleeves and straps from her shoulders down to her elbows, allowing her full breasts to fall free, but she lacked the capacity to gasp. He squeezed her breasts together, his thumbs flicking her hard nipples, but he kept his eyes on her face, gauging her reaction.

Taylor stepped behind her and brought her back against his chest, her clasped hands grazing his thick, hard cock through the denim. He wrapped his arms around her, taking a breast in each hand, and her head fell back onto his shoulder as her eyes flittered closed. He kissed along her outstretched neck up to her ear.

"Do you have any idea how beautiful you are?" but she couldn't speak, her breath a soft hiss through her clenched teeth.

As one hand continued to massage her breast, the other skimmed down her body and pulled the skirt of her dress up until he could reach her hot, wet core. Something between a scream and a growl escaped her throat as he thrust two fingers inside of her. While he twisted her nipple, he pumped his fingers in and out in a slow rhythm and murmured in her ear. "Do you want to feel my cock here? You felt how hard I am, didn't you?" He stroked up to that most sensitive spot, circling it with the lightest caress, then down her cleft and pushed his fingers deep within her again, faster this time. "You can feel my hard cock, how much I want to fuck you. Do you want me to fuck you? Say it. Do you want to feel my cock inside of you?"

After several huffs, she managed to garner enough volume to say, "Yes."

"Yes, what?" He slid his fingers up to work her clit as he continued to nuzzle and kiss her neck and pull her nipple while she writhed against his touch. "I want to hear you say it."

"I want your cock inside of me."

Then he placed his lips against her ear. "Think about my cock inside of you, and come for me, Gillian. Come for me now." Her eyes squeezed tight and she groaned, all of her weight against him, as the sensations of being powerless, completely in his control, flooded through her. "That's it. Come for me, sweetheart."

The climax rolled through her in spasms, curling

her toes as she cried out, jolting her against his chest as his cock threatened to burst through the seams. He didn't cease his sensual ministrations until her convulsions had stopped and she collapsed against him. He pulled his hand out from under her dress and circled both his arms around her waist. "Good girl," he said against her neck between kisses.

Even as he continued to support her spent body against his chest, he finagled the keys out of the pocket of his jeans, tight across his erection, and unlocked the handcuffs, tossing them onto the couch. Once he had her steady on her feet, he pulled her dress back onto her shoulders then walked around to button it up. "How are you?"

She tried to shake off the torpor that had taken hold of her body. "I don't even know. That was…incredible."

He grinned and placed a quick kiss on her lips. "Good. Come on. I have to take you home. Now."

Her brows crinkled over her drowsy eyes. "Why?"

"Because otherwise I'm not going to be able to keep my promise."

Still in a semi-hypnotic state, Gillian slipped on her shoes as Taylor helped her on with her sweater. He tore the door open, blasting them with cold air in stark contrast to the heat they had created. Gillian remained cuddled against him on the short drive to her cabin, then he put the car in park and kissed the top of her head.

"Do you want to come in?"

"You have no idea," he said, "which is why I'm not going to. Unless you want to release me from my promise, I don't even trust myself to walk you to your door. I'm just going to watch you from here then go take the proverbial cold shower."

She chuckled against his arm then sat up. "OK, if you insist." She scooted toward the passenger side door.

"Wait. I have something for you." He bent over to reach under her seat and pulled out the radio.

"What is it?"

"It's the two-way radio. I don't like you being out here by yourself, not able to reach me or for me not to be able to get in touch with you." He turned it on and handed it to her. "Now keep it on this channel, then you just have to hold down this button to talk to me."

"Only you?"

"That's right. Just promise me you'll keep it on."

"I will. Thank you." She placed her free hand against his cheek and pressed her lips upon his for one last, lingering kiss. "Goodnight," she said and opened her door.

"One more thing. What was the message that hate group sent your agent?"

"Oh, uh, not really a message. Just a Bible passage: Revelation two, twenty-one and twenty-two."

They said their final goodnights, and he watched her walk into the cabin then waited until she turned on the light before driving away. He had just crossed his threshold when her voice crackled through the radio in his hand.

"Sam?"

He waited a moment then pressed the button to speak. "Gillian, when you're finished talking, you're supposed to say over. Over."

"Oh. OK. Uh, over."

"Did you need something? Over."

"I just wanted to say thank you.…..Over."

He smiled at the radio. "It was my pleasure. Over."

"I doubt that. I still can't believe you didn't try to…... Over."

"Yeah, neither can I. Over."

"I feel guilty, that you didn't get to…I feel selfish. Over."

"No, sweetheart, I'm the selfish one. You better get some sleep. I have plans for you tomorrow. Over."

"Now I'll never get to sleep. Over." The smile on her voice trickled through the radio.

"It's not going to be easy for me either. Over."

"Sweet dreams, Officer. Over."

"Good night, my sweet. Over and out."

"Over and out."

After setting the radio aside, he found his mother's Bible and turned to the passage Gillian had cited, Revelation 2:21-22.

> *I have given her time to repent of her immorality, but she is unwilling. So I will cast her on a bed of suffering, and I will make those who commit adultery with her suffer intensely, unless they repent of her ways.*

"Jesus Christ."

Chapter 8

Detective Kasey of the 6th Precinct homicide squad arrived at The Metro shortly before one a.m. and identified himself to one of the uniformed officers who stood at the door preventing the patrons from leaving. "Can you take me to the scene?" The officer led him through the dance club, now flooded in bright fluorescent light with no music and the bars no longer serving.

Kasey ducked under the yellow crime tape stretched across the hall entrance leading to the men's room where two fellow investigators had preceded him. "What've we got?" he asked as he walked toward his partner while members of the CSU milled about the cramped space photographing the scene from all angles and collecting evidence.

With his hands on his hips, Detective Reynaud glanced at Kasey then back at the handicap stall. "T.O.D. less than two hours ago. Multiple stab wounds to the back. A lot of blood spray from the victim's mouth, so most likely stabbed in the lungs."

"Drowned in his own blood. Like the others. Witnesses?"

"You kidding? Most of these boys are tweaking. A few said they saw a white male, anywhere from thirty to fifty, medium build, in a knit hat, like a longshoreman, dark jacket over a black hoodie. We're working on getting the security video."

Kasey stepped over to the open stall door and studied the figure prone on the floor in a pool of blood, which had also saturated his shirt. "What're you thinking? Similar to our alley killer, another homosexual male stabbed in the back while on his knees, but now in a men's room."

"If so, this'd be the third in two months."

"But why the change in M.O.?"

"I'm not sure it's the same perp. The motive here could be robbery. No wallet or money on him, and the other victims weren't robbed. I guess we'll know more after the M.E.'s report if it's the same weapon, maybe DNA if we're lucky."

"Well, if it's the same perp, he hasn't worried about leaving DNA. Must know he's not in the system."

"There's something else. Come and look at this."

Kasey walked into the stall to see where his partner pointed at the wall. Amongst all the blood spatter from castoff from the knife, a message had been written in blood:

$$\text{Lev } 20{:}13$$

"Well, that's new."

"We looked it up." As they walked out of the bloody stall, Reynaud read from his notepad. "'If a man has sexual relations with a man as one does with a woman, both of them have done what is detestable. They are to be put to death; their blood will be on their own heads.'"

"So someone comes to a gay bar, lures the victim into the men's room, robs him, stabs him, then writes an anti-gay message in his blood."

"Detectives?" They turned to face the CSU investigator approaching them. "Looks like there's a usable partial print in the message on the wall, so maybe we'll get a hit. Counted seven stab wounds, the weapon had to have a blade at least six inches long."

"That's definitely consistent with the other victims, only they were outside and weren't robbed. Also, fewer stab wounds."

"Here." The CSU handed Kasey an evidence bag with a business card on it. "This is the only thing we found on the victim."

Kasey frowned at the card in the plastic bag. "This is interesting. It's from a robbery detective in Brooklyn."

"You think it's related?" Reynaud asked.

"We'll find out. D'you think it's possible he was robbed *before* tonight?"

The CSU said, "There's something else you need to see." They followed him back but stopped at the stall door. "We didn't find this until we turned him over."

Kasey crouched down to get a better look, careful to stay out of the blood pool. "More like what you didn't find." Reynaud released a high-pitched whistle through his teeth. The index finger of the victim's right hand had been cut off. "I take it you haven't found it anywhere."

"No, sir. We've informed the patrol that's dumpster diving to keep an eye out for a finger as well as the knife."

Kasey peered up at Reynaud with his brows drawn together. "Why cut off his finger? If he was trying to prevent an ID, why only cut off one?"

"Maybe he got interrupted?"

"Trophy maybe?" Kasey pushed his palms down on his thighs to straighten up then glanced back at the message on the wall. "Could have used it to write that."

"If he did, the print'll be useless."

Kasey shook his head. "The overkill, the trophy, the message. This was personal. No way it's the alley killer."

A uniformed officer stepped into the doorway and called out to them, "The manager of the club is here. Do you want to see if he recognizes the deceased?"

"Sure," Reynaud said. "Bring him in."

The officer brought in a petite, fiftyish man with a thin, drawn face and a dyed black crew-cut. "This is the manager, Ben Joy."

"Mr. Joy, do you recognize this man?"

The manager walked toward the last stall then, upon seeing the victim, his eyes bulged, and his hands flew up to cover his mouth as he screeched. "Oh, god! That's Patrick Fitzwilliam!"

The tires of the squad car crunched on the gravel drive leading to Gillian's cabin, drawing her attention from where she sat in jeans and a sweater on the screened front porch with a pen and a notebook. As Chief Taylor walked up to the cabin in full uniform and reflective sunglasses, she set them aside and stood to meet him. The sunset embroiled his silhouette in flames, and she shielded her eyes with her hand as she watched his approach. "Well, hello, Officer. I didn't expect you so early," she said with a grin as he opened the squeaky door, causing her to cringe, then letting it slam behind him. "I swear, every door in this place needs WD-40. Next time I go to town, I've got to get some."

"Hi, Gillian." He used the same official tone and frown he had the first moment she'd laid eyes on him, shadows in the contours of his face mere hints of the dimples revealed when he smiled.

She stepped over to him and rested her hands on his biceps, and he cradled her elbows in his palms as she beamed up at him. "Why don't you ever wear a hat? I always thought a police uniform came with a hat."

He didn't answer, didn't smile. "Gillian, let's go inside. We need to talk."

She dropped her arms and her gaze then turned away from him. "Uh-oh. No good conversation ever started with those four words. Are you breaking up with me after two dates? What is it? I let it get too kinky last night?"

"Gillian." He pulled off his sunglasses just as she glanced back at him, his dark eyes striking her with their resolve. "Let's go inside."

She nodded and hung her head as she stumbled into the cabin through yet another squeaky door with him on her heels. "I…I want you to know, last night…I've never done anything like that before. I haven't even been with a man since my husband left me."

"Gillian, stop talking and sit down."

Unlike at Taylor's cabin, there was no sofa, only two armchairs set far apart from one another, so she sat at the dining table as he walked into the kitchen and opened cabinets. He retrieved a juice glass and filled it to the brim from an open bottle of wine on the counter. Her bottom lip had disappeared into her mouth, her eyes glistening, when he set the glass in front of her. He sat in the adjacent chair, the gold light from the setting sun streaming in through the windows.

When he reached for her hand, she yanked it back but he caught it between both of his and stroked his thumbs across its top. "I have to tell you something."

She tried to wrench her hand free, but he held firm. "Can't you just get it over with? I get it. It's not as if we have a future together anyway. Just say it."

"Look at me." She did, and he gripped her in his stare so she couldn't tear her eyes away. "Sweetheart, this isn't about us. You've gotta know I'm half in love with you already."

"What?"

"It's your friend Jack."

"Jack?"

"He's dead."

"Dead?"

"I am so, so sorry, sweetheart." While holding her in his gaze, he brought her hand to his lips.

The shock cast a pallor over her face like gauze.

"Jack is dead?" He only responded by kissing her hand again. "H-how?"

"He, uh, he was killed. Stabbed."

Tears drifted down her cheeks from the corners of her eyes. "Oh, my god."

"Here." He took away one hand to reach for the glass of wine, which she accepted with robotic movements and brought to her lips, finally breaking free of his stare as she averted her eyes but focusing on nothing.

"It's because of me. It's that Sword of Michael group."

"They don't know that. There have been two similar attacks in the last several weeks, so it's possible it has nothing to do with you."

She took another sip of wine then set the glass aside. "You said possible, not probable. What aren't you telling me?"

He dropped his head and sighed. "There was a Bible verse written on the wall where Jack was found."

"No, no. Jack!" She pulled away, covering her face with her hands as she broke down. Taylor reached for her, but she resisted, shaking her head. "I killed him. This is my fault," she choked out.

"No, it's not your fault. I told you, there were two other men killed just like this before him."

"But what about the Bible verse?"

"It wasn't like the others you've received. It was just one of the same verses those zealots always use. Leviticus twen—"

"Twenty thirteen. Oh god, Sam, I reference that in

the second novel, about hypocrites who call themselves Christians. Th-that can't be a coincidence." Her body wracked with convulsive sobs, and he handed her the handkerchief from his pocket.

Taylor stood and unbuckled his heavy belt, hanging it on the chair, then slid his arms around her back and under her legs to lift her. He carried her to the armchair next to the unlit wood stove and sat down, settling her on his lap, cradling her as if she could ask Santa to bring her Jack for Christmas. As she wept, clinging to his handkerchief, he held her head down against his neck, laying his cheek upon it and stroking her hair. "The only person responsible for this is the man who killed him."

She shook her head against his shoulder. "I-I wish I'd never started this. I'd give up all the money, the success."

He laid kisses on the top of her head. "Jack wanted this for you. He wanted you to be a successful writer."

She lifted her face to meet his eyes, and he wiped a tear from her cheek with his thumb, leaving his palm against her face. "I have hurt so many people. Jack's dead. Sarah's being terrorized. I destroyed my marriage."

"Sarah is fine. And I can't say I'm sorry for that last one." He kissed the tear that rolled out of the corner of her eye then returned his gaze to hers. "I want to kiss all your tears away." He placed his lips against one eyelid then the other, her forehead, her temple.

Gillian shifted on his lap, allowing him to hold her head in both his hands, his eyes tracing her face before he began to cover it with tender kisses, across her cheeks and her jaws. When he reached her mouth, he pressed his lips against it with the same gentleness with no demand; but she moved her lips beneath his in encouragement.

"Hold me. I feel safe in your arms." He lifted his face again to meet her eyes, and she wrapped her arms around his neck, pulling him down against her open mouth and kissing him with ardent urgency. He reciprocated, his arms roaming down her back to bring her tight against him, their tongues rolling around each other as his cock tingled and stiffened under her. Their breaths and heartbeats increased exponentially with their ardor.

He gripped her shoulders and pushed her back. "No, Gillian. I can't do this."

Eyes swollen from crying and lips swollen from their rough kisses, her brows knitted together. "Can't do what?"

"You're overwrought, emotional. You're…you're not in the right state of mind. I can't take advantage of you like this."

"Please take advantage of me." The pleading in her eyes resonated in her voice. "I need to feel human. Take me to bed so I can believe there is still something normal and real in the world. I want to feel you inside me, your life making me feel alive."

He brought his lips down onto hers as he stood up. "I'll bring you to life." Kissing her ravenously, he carried her into the bedroom and laid her on the bed with one knee beside her, leaning over with their arms still around one another, their mouths never parting.

Forcing himself to break away to stand, he never took his gaze from her as he pulled his uniform shirt loose, ripped the snaps apart, and tossed it away. He sat down beside her to divest himself of his boots as she sat up, pulled off her sweater, and unbuttoned her blouse. He yanked his undershirt over his head, leaving him only in his tan slacks and exposing the well-defined muscles beneath the hair on his chest. As her eyes followed the hard lines of his torso and she reached out to touch him, he helped her discard her blouse. She wore a camisole and nothing else underneath, and he kissed her while she kicked off her shoes and unbuttoned her jeans. He slid her jeans down her legs bringing everything with them, including her socks, leaving her only in the blue, silk camisole.

With his erection barreling to get out, he used his kiss to force her down against the pillows then pulled off his slacks and briefs in one swift move. She gaped at his thick, hard cock, at attention and ready for action, then back at his face, his expression as hard and determined as his erection.

Spreading her legs apart, he knelt between her knees, drawing them up and exposing all her wonders to him. He pulled down the top edge of her camisole, freeing her breasts, then she slid the thin straps over and off her arms, which fell back naturally above her head, crossed at the wrists. He kneaded her breasts, teasing the nipples with his thumbs before sucking one and then the other into a stiff peak. While he held one breast for his continued pleasure, she arched her back with a shuddering inhalation as the fingers of his other hand burned a trail of heat down to between her legs. He touched her sensitive nub then dove deep within her, rolling and thrusting in and out, leaving her hot and wet and ready.

He lay on top of her, supporting his weight on his forearms, and pierced her with his eyes. Stroking his hand down her cheek, he offered a short, subtle nod as a question, which she answered with a reciprocal nod.

But the moment his cock nudged against her entrance, she pushed back on his shoulders, forcing his face up enough to meet her wide, panicked eyes.

"Wait," she said.

The head of his cock already nestled in her warm, wet folds, he panted out, "Gillian, this is really not the time."

"I'm sorry, but…condom?"

"I swear to you, I'm clean. You?"

"Yes, but…"

"But what?" He shifted his hips, allowing his shaft to rub against her, causing her lashes to flutter.

"I haven't had sex in over a year."

"God, Gillian, we can discuss the irony of that later, but neither have I."

"Really? But…I don't have birth control."

"It's OK. I've had a vasectomy."

The tension flowing out of her arms and face, she said, "I think I love you," and he plowed into her to the hilt, forcing the air from her lungs. They kissed with fervor, their tongues dancing either when their mouths were glued together or with only the very tips circling as their lips took turns consuming each other in a slow, sensual, erotic waltz keeping time with the rhythmic motion of their bodies. She raised her legs, wrapping them around his waist to take him in deeper. This encouraged him to move faster, the ridge of his glans inside of her creating an intoxicating friction, provoking a soft moan from her with each stroke. She cried out when he lengthened inside of her, and he raised his head and clenched his teeth, groaning as he erupted, filling her with his cum.

He stared down at her peaceful, beatific face and kissed her gently before rolling off of her onto his side and covering them with the blanket before pressing his hand between her legs.

"What are you doing?"

"You didn't come."

"I…I…"

"Don't lie to me. There won't be any 'faking it' with me. I've seen you come, and you haven't yet. I'm about to rectify that."

"But—"

He silenced her by gliding his fingers down her slit, slick with his hot cum, thrusting them inside of her then stroking her clit with his wet touch. She hummed and mewed, wriggling against his touch, her eyes closed and biting down hard enough on her bottom lip it would soon begin to bleed. With one of her arms pinned beneath his body, he gripped her other wrist and squeezed it as tight as he could without breaking it, holding it firm against the bed. He watched her as his fingers moved around her feminine flesh until she threw her head back, opening her mouth and releasing a deep, throaty moan as the ecstasy rippled through her in tremors.

They lay on their sides, and he took both her hands, holding them under his while wrapping his arms around her supple body as she fell asleep. Taylor dozed off and on, whenever waking securing her in his hold. When she awoke, she would have his power and strength supporting her.

After about two hours, she twisted around in his arms, the sadness again shadowing her eyes. Neither spoke, his knuckles skating down her cheek as they gazed into each other's eyes. She pressed her lips to his then a moment later took his flaccid cock in her hand. The shock jerked his head back, his eyes widening as he stared at her, but she said nothing, only stretched up to meet his lips again while stroking the underside of his shaft. As their kisses deepened, the blood rushed to his groin; and once her magical fingers had stiffened his cock, she raised her leg, hooking it over his hip and guiding him inside her.

She caught her breath and closed her eyes with the penetration, but she opened them again as they thrust their hips together. He grew longer and harder inside of her, but then she shifted back, releasing him from her hot, moist sheath, and urged him to lie back on the bed. She crawled down his body, bringing the blanket that had covered them with her, and grasped his cock, still wet with their juices, then rolled her hand up, around, down, around. She met his eyes, his brows raised in pleasant surprise as she twirled the tip of her tongue around the head and ridge, her breath coming in rapid puffs against his turgid flesh. She licked down the vein on the underside of his shaft and back up again, then, with his cock still in her grip, took the head into her mouth with gentle suction. He sank back into the pillows, an arm thrown over his eyes, as she took every inch of him down her throat. With her mouth moving up and down, sucking and licking, soon his hips rose as he released a feral groan, coming in her mouth as she swallowed every drop.

Once his spasms had subsided, she scooted up and curled against his chest, her fingers playing in the hair there as he ran his hand up and down her back. When finally capable of coherent speech, he said, "Not that I'm complaining, but what brought that on?"

"I, um, don't know. I just wanted to. I really never, well. Was it OK?"

He laughed for half a minute before saying, "Yes, sweetheart, that was incredible."

"Good. I don't...I haven't...I'm glad I did it all right."

He chuckled and kissed the top of her head. "That's an understatement. But fucking you...Jesus Christ, that was incredible. I knew it would be."

"How could you know?"

"We bring it out in each other."

They lay in a silent embrace, their fingers intertwined and caressing, their eyes open as if watching their thoughts float by.

"Did you mean what you said before?" he asked.

"What I said when?"

"When you said you thought you loved me."

"Oh! Well, I, uh, was responding to what you had said, the most beautiful words in the world."

"Which were?"

"'I've had a vasectomy.'"

The bed vibrated with his laughter, and she smiled up at him. "If I'd known it was that easy, I'd have gotten it tattooed across my forehead."

"I doubt they'd let you be police chief like that."

"True, but it might be worth it." He kissed her forehead and the tip of her nose then brought their linked hands to his lips and kissed her fingers as he stared in her eyes. "Gillian, I know we've only known each other a few days, but I—"

"Please don't say it," she said, the life and color draining from her face. "I can't think about this right now. Sex is one thing—being in your arms, having the comfort of a physical human connection—but I can't think about you and me, about us...our *relationship*. My best friend was just..." She nestled her head against his chest with a ragged inhalation as her tears rolled down his ribs.

"Shhhh." Releasing her hand, he wrapped his arms around her and tightened his hold as he kissed her hair. "Let me take care of you tonight. Come spend the night at my place."

"Why?"

"Because I have things there that you don't have here."

"Like what?"

"Food, for one thing. But also an old fashioned footed bathtub. Come to my cabin and you can take a hot bubble bath while I cook dinner. Don't worry—I'll keep it strictly physical."

She twisted her neck, resting her chin on his chest, to meet his eyes. "OK."

Chapter 9

The Lord knows how to rescue the godly from temptation, and to keep the unrighteous under punishment for the Day of Judgment, and especially those who indulge the flesh in its corrupt desires.

The Lord God condemned the city of Sodom to destruction and made it an example to those who would live ungodly lives thereafter; and yet He rescued righteous Lot, oppressed by the sensual conduct of unprincipled men—a righteous man but, while living among them, felt his soul tormented day after day by their lawless deeds.

The Sword of Michael the Archangel looked over the gifts the Lord God had bestowed upon him, rewards for efforts to find this Jezebel, the one with eyes full of adultery that never cease from sin, enticing unstable souls, having a heart trained in greed. For speaking out arrogant words of vanity, she entices by fleshly desires, by sensuality, those who barely escape from the ones who live in error, promising them freedom while she is a slave of corruption; for by what a man is overcome, by this he is enslaved. For if, after he has escaped the defilements of the world by the knowledge of the Lord and Savior Jesus Christ, he is again entangled in them and overcome, the last state has become worse for him than the first.

Like the angels who had disguised themselves as men in Sodom at the house of Lot, the Sword of Michael the Archangel had descended into the den of iniquity to receive these gifts from God. These sodomites, like unreasoning animals, born as creatures of instinct to be captured and killed, will in the destruction of those creatures also be destroyed, suffering wrong as the wages of doing wrong. They are stains and blemishes, reveling in their deceptions, as they carouse with you. Daring, self-willed, they do not tremble when they revile angelic majesties—angels who are greater in might and power.

And the Lord God with these gifts had delivered onto the Sword of Michael the Archangel the Jezebel.

"Hi Jack. Do you listen to *your* voice mail? For your information, I did not do anything. Someone broke into Sarah's house, and they thought it might be related to the hate mail I've been getting. Love the cabin, by the way. *Lake Kiwassa* is amazing...."

With her blood spattered on the wall, they will find no more of her than the skull and the feet and the palms of her hands.

For it would be better for them not to have known the way of righteousness, than having known it, to turn away from the holy commandment handed on to them.

❧

They spoke little in their haste to leave Jack's parents' cabin. As Taylor put on his uniform, Gillian threw on a dress then stuffed socks, a nightshirt, and her toothbrush into the tote bag with her notebook. She had pulled on her long sweater, but by the time Taylor opened the door, the temperature outside had dropped substantially; so he yanked her coat from the hook and helped her on with it. Just before walking out, she grabbed two bottles of wine to bring along.

Gillian sat on the edge of the tub in Taylor's cabin as it filled with hot, bubbly water, skimming her fingers through it while staring at nothing on the wall, sadness ingrained on her features. She turned to face Taylor when he walked in with towels and a bathrobe.

"I hope you like spaghetti carbonara," he said. "I guess I kind of exaggerated on the food."

"Thanks, it sounds great, but don't go to the trouble. I'm really not hungry."

"Well, the water's already on to boil, and you're going to eat it regardless. When was the last time you had anything to eat?"

She looked down at her fingers in the water, shaking her head. "I don't know." She started and her spine straightened when he began to lower the zipper on the back of her dress.

He rubbed her bare back a few moments then kissed the side of her neck. "Go ahead and get in the tub, and I'll bring you a glass of wine."

She had just slid into the steaming water when he came in and handed her the glass. He rolled a hand

115

towel and placed it on the edge of the tub then pulled her back to rest her neck against it, her eyes rolling up to see him upside down staring at her.

"You just relax, and I'll be back in a few minutes."

When he returned, he had changed out of his uniform into jeans and a t-shirt. He knelt on a bathmat at the end of the tub then had her sit up and set her wine glass on the floor. He washed her hair, massaging her scalp then down her neck and deep into her shoulders, her eyes closing with her deep exhalation as her muscles relaxed under the pressure of his thumbs and fingers. As the bubbles dissipated, she bent her knees and wrapped her arms around her legs, and he rinsed her hair with the hand shower attached to the faucet of the claw foot tub.

Taylor stood and turned off the water then lifted her chin, raising her frowning face to meet her red-rimmed eyes. "I'm going to go finish cooking dinner while you dry off. Then put on the robe and go sit on the couch. I lit the fire in the stove to warm you up. And don't forget your wine." She nodded, and he bent down and pressed his lips onto hers with a sweet, gentle kiss before leaving her alone.

When Taylor met her in the living room, he held a large bowl of pasta on a napkin in one hand and a glass of wine in the other. Setting his glass on the coffee table next to hers, he sat down on the couch close to her. He twirled a few strands of spaghetti on the one fork then brought it to her mouth.

"What are you doing?" she asked.

"I'm feeding you. Otherwise you'll just push it around on your plate and only take two bites. Now open."

She opened her mouth to accept the forkful of pasta. As she ate it, he gathered more spaghetti on the fork, eating from the same bowl. "It's wonderful," she said after swallowing and taking a sip of wine.

He had another bite ready for her. "Open." After sliding the pasta into her mouth, he said, "Tell me about Jack. How did you meet him?" He ate again while waiting for her to answer.

"At a romance novel convention. We were sat together at one of the dinners and just got to talking, hit it off immediately."

They continued to eat, with him feeding her, and talk about Jack, stopping only so he could bring in more wine. She shed a few tears, which he wiped away, but also smiled at some of the remembrances.

After a while, she held up her hand. "No, really, I can't eat another bite. I'm getting full."

"All right, I suppose you've eaten enough."

She rested her head against the back of the couch, gazing at him. "Why are you doing this?"

"Doing what?"

"Being so nice to me. Pampering me, feeding me."

"I told you." He set the dish on the table and took her into his arms, holding her head against his chest. "I want to take care of you."

"But why?"

"Because you need me."

His heart beat beneath her cheek as he brushed his hand down her damp curls.

"I'm scared," she said.

"I know."

"I don't mean about the threats."

"I know."

Gillian sat in her car in the middle of town crying with Sarah's sobs seeping through the cell phone against her ear.

"I know I only met him a couple of times," Sarah said, "but I did really like him. And I know how close you two were—plus look what he's done for your career."

Gillian covered her eyes with her hand. "Yeah, but it was probably this *career* that got him killed."

"We don't know that for sure, but…I do have to tell you something. I'm sorry, Gillian, but I can't represent you anymore. At least not until they catch whoever is doing this."

"Oh, Sarah." She set her cell phone aside as she choked on her tears. Once she had stifled her emotions enough to speak, she lifted the phone to her ear. "I'm so sorry, but I understand."

"The detective that contacted me about Jack, the same one investigating my break-in, said it's possible whoever did this is trying to hurt you by…hurting people close to you."

"Oh, my god. So they're sure it's related? Sam said there was a chance it was someone who had already killed two other people."

"Who is Sam?"

"He's, uh, the police chief I mentioned to you."

"Uh-huh. Well, they haven't completely ruled that

out, but the police said this seemed more personal because it was overk—"

"Over what?"

"Gillian, you really don't want to know the grisly details."

She threw her head back against the car seat. "Fucking hell! *Grisly?* His poor parents. Do they even know? They're on a cruise somewhere."

"They're coming back next week. The police are holding off notification until then, so the funeral won't be for a while. When are you coming back?"

She shrugged and shook her head even though Sarah couldn't see. "I don't know. I don't feel safe going to my apartment, but I can't keep staying in his parents' cabin. It makes me feel even more guilty."

"Listen, I'm going to go stay at my mother's in Paramus for a few days, maybe until they figure out who did this. Why don't you come down and stay with us. You know she's always liked you."

"Even after I wrote these kinky books?"

"I, uh…yeah. I never told her that you're P.G. Tate. Anyway, no one would think to look for you there."

"Is that why you're going? Are you afraid Jack's killer will come after you?"

"I don't know what to think, but I'm alone a lot, working from home with Jacob gone most of the time. He's been working a case in Boston, and he said he might have to stay over tomorrow night. I just don't want to be by myself right now."

"I know what you mean."

"So what's going on with you and Sam the police chief?"

"I don't know. It's complicated. If you're sure your mom really won't mind, I think I will join you, even though it is New Jersey."

"Good. It'll be a relief to know you're safe. You probably need to tell your other friends and family what's going on."

She closed her eyes and let her breath ripple through her lips. "I guess you're right."

"By the way, I do have some good news. First of all, because of Jack's death, the publisher has extended your deadline by two weeks."

"Well, I guess that's something. They were his publisher, too."

"And, secondly, sales of *Pricked with Thorns* have gone through the roof. You've already surpassed the sales of *Petals*."

"Wow. MMF really does sell well."

"There's even a rumor that you're really a gay man because the sex scenes are so authentic."

"But people have seen me. Yes, in a red wig, but I've been interviewed on TV. How could I pull that off if I were a man?"

"I don't know. Look at Lady Gaga."

Gillian smiled. "Please don't make me laugh. I'm too sad to laugh."

"Jack would want you to laugh. So when will you be coming down?"

"I'll head on back to the cabin and start packing now, but I'm not up for another five hour drive. I'll stop somewhere along the way, maybe Saratoga, and join you tomorrow. I think I need a night alone anyway."

"What about the police chief?"

"Yeah…He's working today. I've got to get out of here before he has a chance to stop me."

"You're not even going to tell him goodbye?"

"I told you, it's complicated. But it has helped me come up with a title for the third novel."

"What is it?"

"*A Bed of Nails and Roses*."

After hanging up, Gillian called her daughters to tell them about Jack and the Sword of Michael the Archangel. Her daughter at Georgetown thought she was fine staying put, but Gillian finally convinced the one in Manhattan to stay with friends.

Then she took a deep breath, blew it out, and called her ex-husband.

A woman answered, screaming, "You fucking bitch!"

Gillian flinched then glanced at her cell phone screen. It indicated she had indeed dialed Martin. "I'm sorry, I was trying to reach Martin Tate. Is this still his number?"

"You know goddamn well it is. You have some nerve calling him after what you've put him through. You have no right! You are divorced! D-I-V-O-R-C-E-D!"

"Thank you. I've always wondered how that was spelled. I take it you must be Linda."

"It's Glenda, and you damn well know it!"

"Would you please put Martin on the phone?"

"I will not. He is livid. LIVID!"

"Would you mind spelling that for me as well?"

"He is furious that you named one of the characters

in your new novel 'Martin.'"

Gillian rubbed her eyes and sighed. "Why? Are people now accusing him of being gay? He knows exactly why I named the character Martin. Would you please put him on the phone?"

"He doesn't want to talk to you."

"So stipulated for the record. Listen, Lin-*Glen*da, I don't want to talk to him either, but it's important."

"He's in the shower anyway. Whatever you have to say to him, you can tell me."

"Oh, for fuck's sake. Fine. There's this group—a hate group—The Sword of Michael the Archangel."

"What are you talking about, 'the Sword'?"

"Hey, I didn't name them. They've been sending me harassing emails and letters with all these passages from the Bible."

"Well, you brought that on yourself!"

Gillian wiped her hand down her face and turned her eyes to the ceiling of the car. "Listen. Would you please tell Martin that Jack was murdered, and there is a slim possibility that it could be related to this Sword of Michael group, and the killer might go after other people associated with me?"

"Oh, great! So now on top of everything else, you've put his life in danger?"

"And, other than having a gay character with the same name as his, what have I done to him exactly? He's the one who left me!"

"How could he stay married to you and teach at King's while you're putting out all that smut?"

"That was his choice to tell them that I'm P.—Oh, what the hell am I doing? I am not going to defend myself. I made him a multimillionaire! He didn't even need to work anywhere. And tell me this, were you fucking my husband while we were still married?"

"That is none of your business!"

"Oh. Right. I was just his wife!"

"And soon *I* am going to be his wife. We're engaged now."

"Good. You deserve each other. Look, I just called to warn him about what happened to Jack."

"Well, he's getting ready to go to Philadelphia for a conference anyway."

Gillian could hear Martin's voice in the background. *"Who are you talking to?"*

"*Now* can I talk to him?" Gillian asked.

"I told you I'd give him the message, that you might have gotten a psycho-killer after him."

"You better watch yourself, too, Glenda, or someone might drop a house on you!"

Gillian pressed the button to end the call with extra force then tossed the phone upon the passenger's seat. Her fingers shook as she started the engine, so she dropped her head against her hands where they held onto the steering wheel. Once she had collected herself enough to drive, she shifted into reverse and backed away.

Chapter 10

Gillian rushed from room to room in the small cabin, stripping the sheets off the bed and putting them with all the towels in the washer as she went about packing and cleaning. By the time the linens were dry, the sun had begun to set, shedding an orange glow throughout the cabin. She had everything else done, her car packed and ready to go. When she put the sheets back on the bed, she smoothed her hand over them with a slow wistfulness then glanced at the two-way radio on the dresser.

After she finished making the bed, she walked over and picked up the radio, staring at it as her quickened pulse and breaths tightened around her throat. Her eyes brimmed with tears and she swallowed. After one more pass through the cabin with the radio still in her hand, she put on her coat and stepped out onto the deck, peering out at the lake, her breath visible in the cool air.

She raised her eyes to heaven then took a deep breath and pressed the button to talk.

"Sam?" she said, released the button then pressed it again just long enough to say, "Over."

"Hi, Gillian. I was just thinking about you. How're you doing? Over."

She held the talk button down, which prevented him from being able to respond as she spoke. "I'm leaving, Sam. I can't stay here with everything that's going on. It's all just…too much. I don't know how to handle any of this, with Jack, with…you. I just didn't want to leave without telling you goodbye and thanking you for taking care of me last night. I…I have to go now. Over and out."

She turned the radio off.

When she drove toward the road to town, Gillian pulled over at Taylor's cabin and parked. She jumped out of her car with the two-way and left it on his front porch by the door. As she shifted her car into reverse, Taylor's patrol car drove up, and he parked it across the drive, blocking her in. She caught a glimpse of him walking toward her in the rearview mirror wearing his uniform and a police jacket, then she crossed her arms across the steering wheel and laid her head down, drying her tears on the sleeve of her coat.

He tapped on her window with his nightstick. "Roll down your window and turn off the engine," he said with an authority that would not be broached. She straightened up and did as he instructed but with her eyes directed forward. "What the hell do you think you're doing?"

"I was just leaving the two-way for you."

"You know what I'm talking about. Why the hell are you leaving? And you're just going to drop a bomb on me like that over the radio and then run off? I don't think so."

"My best friend is dead, my friends and family are in danger. I can't just hide up here."

"And what about us?"

She shook her head. "That's why I have to go now. There is no 'us.' There can't be an 'us.'"

"Goddamnit, look at me, Gillian!" He thumped the roof of the car with the bottom of his nightstick, and she jumped. She turned to him with shining bloodshot eyes as he leaned into the window. "Why can't there be an 'us'?"

"Our lives are just too different. You're the police chief in this tiny town up here practically in Canada. I live in the City, and I have this writing career that has me traveling all over the world. I can't stay here. I need to leave before we get in too deep."

"I hate to tell you this, sweetheart, but we already are in deep."

She closed her eyes tight, forcing a few tears through her lashes. "Don't you see there's no future for us?"

He reached in and wiped the tears off one cheek with his thumb. "I know you struggle with this, but we should just be in the present and see where this leads us; let the future take care of itself."

"I just can't live like that, lying to myself when I know this could only end badly."

"You don't know that."

"How could it not? I can't stay here. And I can't stay in that cabin anymore. Jack's dead, and his parents don't even know it, and I'm in *their* cabin."

"You can stay here in my cabin."

She opened her eyes, gaping at him as she shook

her head. "This is what I'm talking about. This is moving too fast. We just met. Now you're suggesting that we live together?"

He stood back and glanced down the lake from where she had come. "You know, all these other cabins are vacant. I'm sure one of the owners would love to have someone rent a cabin in the off season." He turned to her, his eyes landing on her hands gripping the steering wheel so tight, her knuckles were white. "Gillian, I know it's fast, but I also know what's happening here. Can you honestly tell me you don't feel it, too?"

"It doesn't matter."

"Can you tell me that?"

"Can you tell me one reason why you think we might have a future together?"

Leaning against the roof of her car, he turned facing the lake, almost black with the descent of the sun. He stood up straight and took a step back, then she dropped her head and reached to start her engine.

"Ma'am," he said, his tone harsh. "Please take your keys out of the ignition and step out of the vehicle."

She froze, her fingers still on the key, only her eyes flitting in confused circles.

"I said, remove your keys from the ignition and step out of the vehicle."

Her heart rate climbing, she pulled out the keys, laid them on the dash, then opened her door and climbed out of the car. She crossed her arms and frowned at him. "What are you doing?"

"Take off your coat and leave it on your seat."

"Won't I be cold?"

"Not for long. Now leave your coat in the car and step away from the vehicle."

With her eyes on him as he watched her every movement, tapping his nightstick against his palm, she unbuttoned her coat then let it slide off and tossed it onto the seat behind her.

"Now go to the front of the vehicle and assume the position."

"What's 'the position'?"

He gripped her arm and led her around the open door then released her. "Bend over with your palms flat on the hood and spread your legs."

She remained still a moment, biting her bottom lip as they stood there in the silence of the night with the only light coming from inside her car. Her short puffs of air forming a soft fog with each quick breath, she bent over and placed her hands down on the hood, barely warm from her brief drive.

"Spread your legs wider." He ran the nightstick up the inside of one leg all the way up her skirt to where her thighs met and then down the other leg, tapping it until she widened her stance.

He unzipped his jacket and tossed it with the nightstick on top of Gillian's coat then walked back to where she remained against her car, completely still except for the steady rise and fall of her back with her respiration, and he stretched over her on the hood with his mouth behind her ear. "I'm going to frisk you now," he said on a soft breath, his own breathing becoming more heavy and shallow. He placed his hands on top of hers then circled his fingers around her wrists and continued up her arms at a deliberate pace.

He reached her shoulders, and then, with his cheek against hers, his hands roamed down the front of her dress, over her breasts. She again wore a dress with buttons down the front, and he began opening them, her eyes closing as a rasping breath rose from her throat.

"I have to check for concealed weapons," he said low against her cheek, his voice gruff as his fingers traced over the hardened nipples then slipped under the lace to touch them, and her head fell forward with a groan. He continued with his thorough search, his hands running down and around her torso, back, and sides. He crouched down and wrapped his fingers around her ankles then, as he rose steadily, he brought his hands up her skirt against the bare skin of her soft thighs. He pressed his face against hers again when he reached her ass, and he drew one hand down to between her legs. Her head fell back against his shoulder with a low moan as his fingers rubbed against the wet lips. "You remembered, didn't you? I don't like you wearing anything under your skirts," he said against her throat. "And you obeyed."

"Yes," she whispered.

"Good. Then I can touch you. I love to feel you wet like this, how much you want my cock." He easily slipped his fingers inside of her, the shock of the pleasure overwhelming her, and she fell against the hood of the car, one side of her face flat against it, bent over, open and ready for him.

Pulling the skirt of her dress up onto her back, he withdrew his hand from between her legs and smoothed his palm over the sumptuous curves of her ass. He raised his hand and brought it flat down on her right cheek with a resounding *thwack*. She jumped and gasped but didn't protest. He kept his eyes on her as he caressed the sting out of the red hand impression.

"I told you never turn off that radio."

Then he slapped her other cheek, and a slight smile rose from the corner of her mouth on her blissful face. He spanked her several more times, the sounds echoing through the woods, pausing after each impact to rub away the burn, until her ass was red and hot.

"I think you've had enough of that...for now."

Taylor ran his hand down to where her thighs met. His teeth clenched and his thick erection pressing against his slacks, he watched his fingers pumping in and out of her tight, drenching core, as she mewled and pushed back against his hand. He used his other hand to release his police belt, letting it slide to the ground, then pulled down his zipper to free his hard-on.

He leaned over her with his face close to hers. "Is that what you want?"

"Yes," she said on a sigh.

"Yes, what?"

"I want you to fuck me."

He rolled his fingers inside of her, eliciting a guttural whimper. "Like this? You want me to finger fuck you?"

"Mmmm...No."

"Then say it. Tell me what you want."

She opened her eyes and met his gaze directly, although she had to force her words out with her labored breaths. "I want your cock. I want to feel your hard cock inside of me. I want you to fuck me."

"Out here?"

"Yes," she murmured, her lashes fluttering. "Here, now, please. Fuck me hard."

He straightened and moved between her legs, pulled out his fingers and plunged his cock into her, deep and hard. She cried out with the welcome invasion, raising her head and closing her eyes, then grinding her hips back to meet him. With each thrust, he pulled out farther just to drive in deeper. The ridge of his glans gliding across her tight sheath from that angle, with the head of his cock striking that one particular spot, she groaned as she teetered on the edge.

He stretched down to lean forward and spoke low and rough in her ear. "Is this reason enough for you?" But he had rendered her incapable of speech, only able to huff out feral sounds of rapture. He reached his hand, still wet from her juices, around to her clit, teasing and circling it with his fingers until she came in violent spasms and screamed out her delight.

With his hands on her hips, he grimaced as he mustered all of his self-control to break the magnetic suction of her heat and force his erect cock out, pushing it back into his slacks, pulling her skirt down over her, then picking up his belt. Still in the throes of the aftermath of her orgasm, she paid no attention as he clipped on his belt and pulled out the handcuffs.

"I'm going to have to take you in," he said, bringing one hand behind her back and clicking the cuff around her wrist. She stood up, her features sleepy and confused, as he attached the handcuffs to her other wrist behind her back then grasped her arm to usher her along.

"Wha-what are you doing?"

"I told you, I'm taking you in." He slammed her car door shut as he marched her toward his cabin and up the porch steps.

"Why?"

When they reached the door, he unlocked it then let his mouth brush against her ear. "Because I haven't finished yet. I still need to fill you with my cum. I want to kiss you until your lips are raw. I want to see you on your knees sucking my cock. I want to touch and lick every inch of you. I want you lying naked across my bed when I fuck you. And I want to make you come until you're begging me to stop."

He lifted his head to see her face—flushed but with a burgeoning smile and a spark in her eyes. With a combination of lust and relief, he threaded his fingers in her hair and brought her mouth to his with a kiss full of promise of things to come.

Chapter 11

"It's definitely your alley killer."

"You're shitting me," Kasey said to the medical examiner then glanced up at his partner.

"I shit you not," Dr. Bernard said. "Unless you have two killers using the same murder weapon, with the same force and depth."

"Any chance of getting DNA?" Reynaud asked.

"Just like with the others, there was definitely semen in the victim's mouth."

Kasey grimaced. "Geez, Doc, I never get tired of hearing you say that."

"Of course, the victim aspirated his own blood, so they'll have to separate the DNA during the analysis, but there's a good chance they'll be able to get a sample that we can use to compare to the suspect in the other homicides. Maybe next week."

"What about the finger?"

"Severed through the proximal phalanx of the right index finger. I'd say the assailant held the victim's hand down and delivered a single downward blow, most likely with the murder weapon. Perimortem."

"Damn. He was alive when he had his finger

chopped off?"

"Technically, but he most likely was in shock."

"Plus he was probably kinda distracted by being stabbed in the back seven times," Reynaud said.

"Eight, actually," said the doctor.

"So if it's the same killer," Kasey said, "why so many more stab wounds?"

"Public place, maybe wanted him to die quicker."

"Any hypothesis on the finger?"

"No, but based on the swirl patterns of the remaining digits, the fingerprint analyst said it's unlikely it was used to write the message on the wall. You may very well have a fingerprint of the killer now."

"Good. Now we just need to find a print that matches."

"Probably ought to let that detective in Brooklyn know," Reynaud said, "maybe get them to put a rush on processing those prints from the burglary so we can rule out a connection."

"Or confirm it."

"Aren't you going to be late for work?" Gillian gleamed up at Taylor from where she lay against him, her head in the crook of his arm.

"I don't have another shift until Sunday." Tangled with her in the sheets of his bed, the morning light sneaking in through the break in the curtains, he held her right hand in his left and pressed his lips along the chaffing on her wrist from their activities of the night before. "I don't want to use those handcuffs on you anymore," he said between kisses. "They're too rough on you."

"I don't mind," she said with a grin.

"But I do." Then he shifted his focus from her hand to her face. "Does this mean you've given up that ludicrous idea of running off to New Jersey?" He kissed her forehead and the tip of her nose.

"Yes, but…"

"Uh-oh. 'But' can never be good."

"But I can't stay here forever. And all my reasons for leaving still exist. Mind-blowing sex and dominance and bondage and fulfilling my fantasies is no basis for a permanent relationship."

He arched an eyebrow with his crooked smile. "I don't know. Sounds pretty good to me."

Although she laughed, she resisted when he tried to enfold her in his arms and pulled back. "You know what I mean."

On his side with his head against his fist supported by his arm, Taylor gazed down at her and traced her hairline with his finger. "There's something wrong with your logic, sweetheart. If the only thing we have between us is that you like to be tied up and I like to do it, and you say that's no basis for a relationship, then why would you be worried about the future?"

"Because…" She glanced downward for a moment then back to his eyes. "Because I'm afraid of falling in love with you."

Caressing her bottom lip with his thumb, he said, "I'm already in love with you."

She closed her eyes and shook her head. "No, don't

say that. You can't be."

He stilled her by placing his hand upon her cheek, and she looked up at him. "I am, Gillian. I love being with you. I love taking care of you. I love that you talk dirty in bed. I love fucking you, and I love hearing you say that you want me to fuck you. I love thinking about you when we're not even together, which I have been doing since the moment I handed you that can of chili. You're just going to have to accept it. I am in love with you."

"You don't even know me. We've spent, what? Five evenings together?"

"I know couples who have gotten married after far less."

She flung herself forward to sit straight up in bed. "Married!"

"That wasn't a proposal; it was just an observation."

"Oh." Blowing out a sigh of relief, she flopped back down flat on the bed. "Thank heaven for that!"

"Well, you don't have to make it sound like marriage to me would be *that* absurd."

She covered her eyes with her arm. "I don't want to get married again to *anyone*, but after only five days, yes, it would be absurd."

"But I also know you from reading your book."

"What are you talking about? That's fiction."

"I know, and I know it's not autobiographical, but I see you in Em."

"I'm nothing like Em."

"In the fundamentals, no, but I could sift through all that and find the truth about you. Like wanting to be tied up. Wanting a man strong enough to dominate her and take control. And her need to be wanted. That's why she sleeps with two men at once, to make her feel desirable. But she really needs someone to take care of her when the chaos of the world overwhelms her. That's when I knew I could be that for you. Jesus, more men should read romance novels. That's when I realized for the first time what I had always wanted, what had been the missing piece in my past relationships. I knew you were the woman I had been waiting for, my missing piece, that you and I would fit."

Even with her arm slung across her eyes, as he spoke, a few tears had trickled down her temple and dampened the sheet. "She's just a character in a novel. I'm not Em."

"Gillian, even her name—Em. It's 'me' spelled backwards."

"Oh, my god." She sat up and cradled her head in her hands, silently crying into her palms. "I didn't even realize that."

Taylor knelt beside her and rubbed her back. "You mean you didn't do that on purpose?"

"No, I chose the names from a Jane Austen book. No wonder Martin thought that I wanted another man."

"You didn't want another man in bed with Martin. You needed a different man. I know I'm only one man, but I can show you every day how much you are wanted, desired. I want someone who needs me, and you need somewhat who wants you."

When he wrapped his arms around her, she did not

resist this time but clung to him. "What am I going to do? What am I going to do?"

"Shhhhh….It's OK." He lifted her face to meet his eyes. "Just let me love you."

A sob shuddered through her as she gazed at him with wet, red eyes. "I can't stay here."

"This is what we're going to do. You're going to go splash water on your face or shower or whatever and throw on one of those dresses that make me crazy, then we're going to go into town and have breakfast— in a restaurant, or at least a diner, like a real date— because I am famished."

"And I need to call Sarah and let her know if I'm not going to Paramus."

"You're not going to Paramus, even if I have to put you across my knee and give you a spanking." Biting her bottom lip with a trace of a smile, she blushed and averted her eyes. He grinned and kissed her forehead. "Besides, you still owe me a dance. We will find the owner of one of these other cabins to rent and get you settled in there so you can finish your book while we spend more time 'getting acquainted.'"

"And after that?"

"You know, there is such a thing as long-distant relationships, and five hours isn't *that* far."

"I don't want that."

"Neither do I, my love. We'll just take it one step at a time. But first…" He swept a hand down her bare body. "I think I better fuck you again."

Following along Taylor's laid out plan, they arrived at the busy diner in town closer to lunchtime, but they still ordered breakfast and coffee. As police chief, his presence there with an unfamiliar woman drew the attention of most of the other diners, and Gillian fidgeted in her seat under their perusal.

"What's the matter? I'd think you'd be used to being the center of attention."

"That's P.G. Tate. I'm certainly not, especially as the strange woman with the police chief. Which reminds me, I need to call my agent, or former agent rather, and let her know I'm not coming."

Gillian dug in her purse for her phone then turned it on. Once it had powered up, she pressed the tip of her forefinger on the button, and her home screen appeared.

"What are you doing there?" Taylor asked.

"What do you mean?"

"Pressing your finger on the phone like that."

"Oh. It has touch ID. Instead of using a passcode, it just recognizes my fingerprint. You haven't seen that before?"

"No, but it did give me an idea about this case. After we eat, I need to stop by the police station."

She didn't respond as she focused on her reunion with technology. "Oh, a text from Sarah. Paramus is off anyway. Her husband isn't going to Boston after all, so she wants me to stay with them in Brooklyn. That's not happening!" Her thumbs tapped out a text reply to Sarah. "But I still have to find a different cabin."

"And you won't just stay with me."

"That would be tantamount to living together. We've only known each other a few days."

"And? What better way to get better acquainted?"

She widened her eyes with feigned shock. "Why, Chief Taylor! What kind of example would you be setting for the town if you were living in sin? Besides, I need my own space. If I'm going to be staying here a few weeks, I need a writer's cave where I can spread out and be messy and eat ravioli and not have to worry about disturbing someone's stuff."

"All right. I get it. But I expect plenty of sleepovers."

As they were leaving, the bell on the door jangled as he opened it for her. "When we get to the police station, maybe there's a computer I could use to find another cabin?"

"Or we could stop by my place here in town," he said as he followed her out.

"Really? I actually get to see the inner sanctum?"

"Well, it has been a few days. I really should check on the girl in the pit."

She giggled and knocked her side against his, and he wrapped his arm around her waist.

"Hey, Chief, we didn't expect to see you today," said a uniformed officer when Taylor ushered Gillian into the police station, a proprietary hand on her back.

"Gillian, this is Sergeant Williams, Sergeant James," Taylor said, nodding at each man in turn as they rose from behind their desks. "This is Gillian Tate. You remember the report we got on threats she was receiving."

"Glad to know you," James said as both men approached and shook her hand. "Have you received more threats while you've been at the lake?"

"Uh, not me, personally," she said.

"She wants to move to a different cabin," Taylor said as he helped her off with her coat. "I need to go in my office and make some calls. Williams, could you get her logged onto a computer or help her find one she can rent for a few weeks?"

"Sure thing. Right this way, Mrs. Tate."

"G-Gillian. Please just call me Gillian."

In his office, Taylor had a full view of the squad room through the plate glass window that encompassed the front wall, and he stood, waiting until the sergeant had Gillian settled behind a desk before dialing the number for the NYPD 68th Precinct.

"Bennet."

"Detective Bennet, it's Sam Taylor."

"Chief Taylor. I was going to be calling you soon. What's up?"

"It's about Jack Clifford. I have a hunch about the severed finger."

"That's one piece of the puzzle the homicide detectives haven't been able to figure out. Whatcha got?"

"Did they find his cell phone on his body? The assailant could have used the severed finger to access the victim's cell phone with his fingerprint and locate Gillian. Ms. Tate."

"Well, there's an idea, and as far as I know, they didn't find anything on him—except my card—but the medical examiner has confirmed that Mr. Clifford and the other two victims were all killed by the same assailant."

Taylor ran his hand down his face as he released a full, audible breath. "So there's no connection between his death and Ms. Tate." He glanced over to Gillian with love and relief softening his eyes.

"Seems highly unlikely. Also, they found a viable fingerprint at the crime scene, so they'll have a solid ID once they have a suspect in custody."

"That's good news. I know Ms. Tate will be glad to hear they're close to catching his killer."

"Yeah, I'm just waiting for them to rule out all of the prints collected from the Falgert robbery, then I was going to call you."

"I appreciate that. Even though it's unrelated to the murders, I would like to find this Sword of Michael group that's been harassing her."

Sitting behind the computer, Gillian had her cell phone on her ear, and she finished her call as Taylor and Detective Bennet wrapped up. She stood, glancing up at him just as he opened his office door and walked toward her, the corners of both their mouths rising.

"I found a cabin," she said when they reached one another.

"That's good. I have something to tell you. Let's go to the interview room so we can talk in private."

"Not your office?"

"You kidding? That's like being in a fishbowl." The heads of both sergeants and a patrolman turned to watch as Taylor led her to the interview room with his hand between her shoulder blades.

Once he had closed the door, she turned to him with

worry widening her eyes. "What's wrong?"

He ran his hands along her upper arms and smiled down at her. "Nothing. It's good news. I just spoke with the detective in Brooklyn, and the medical examiner determined that Jack was killed by the same man who killed the other two victims over the last few weeks."

"So what does that mean?"

"That it's highly unlikely his death had anything to do with you."

Relief poured over her and flooded her eyes, and she flung herself against his chest as he pulled her into his arms. "Oh, thank god. I don't know how I could face his parents if I were responsible for his death."

"I keep telling you, even if it had been related to your books or those threats, you still wouldn't be responsible for the actions of some fanatic. And something else, too. They have a good fingerprint, so they're getting closer to finding the psycho-killer who really is responsible."

"Th-that's good. I want the bastard to pay for this, but it still won't bring Jack back."

He rubbed her back and kissed the top of her head. "I know."

"Why didn't you want to tell me in your office?"

"Well, because I couldn't be holding you like I am now, and I certainly couldn't do this." He tilted his face down as he lifted her chin and kissed her. Then he kissed her again, and she wrapped her arms around his neck to pull their mouths closer together. "I don't suppose you have any fantasies in an interrogation room, huh?"

She grinned against his lips. "Not yet, but I'm getting some ideas."

After one last kiss, he withdrew but held her hands and brought her wrists to his lips. "So where's this cabin?"

"I think it's two cabins up from Jack's."

"Well, at least it'll be a little closer to mine, but you have to promise never to turn off the two-way again. Got it?"

"I promise, I never will. I need to go get the keys and pay the owner."

"OK, I'll help you get settled into your new digs, but then I have a quick errand."

"And how 'bout I fix dinner for you tonight?"

"Uh-oh. Beef stew or canned tamales?"

"Do you like chili dogs?"

Chapter 12

Kasey and Reynaud sat at their desks across from each other passing a miniature basketball back and forth as they bounced ideas around.

"So we've got surveillance footage from near the first two crime scenes that could definitely be a longshoreman hat and jacket."

"But no facial recognition. He definitely knew to hide from the cameras."

"Matches the description from the witnesses at the disco."

"Disco?"

"Whatever. Doesn't matter. Can't stop every guy in a hat and ask for DNA."

"OK. First this guy has the vic blow him, and then he kills him."

"So he's either a self-hating homosexual or a psychotic homophobe."

"Hey, are you gay?"

"What're you talking about?"

"Would you let some guy suck your dick?"

"Why don't you blow me? Fuck, no! But I'm also not a psychopathic killer."

"I think we're looking for a gay homophobe."

"Like self-loathing? In denial—in the closet."

"And what? He's got so much to lose if he's outed, he kills the guy who blows him to get rid of witnesses?"

"All right, let's look at the first two victims."

Kasey caught the ball and held it. "No, let's look at the *last* victim. Why would the perp risk discovery by being in a public place and staying at the scene at least twice as long as in the alleys? Think about it. Stabs him twice as many times as the others, steals his wallet, writes a message on the wall, and cuts off his finger."

"And don't forget the blow job."

"Believe me, I'd like to. He spent a lot of time there when someone could have walked in."

Reynaud's eyes remained on the ball as Kasey twisted it in his hands for several thoughtful moments. Then he raised his head and gawked at Kasey, who began nodding when he met his eyes.

"Clifford was always the primary target. The others were just substitutes."

Kasey tossed him the ball. "Exactamundo. We've had the victimology backwards."

"So we need to focus on Jack Clifford. *He's* the important victim. Motive?"

"Remember, he's not just Jack Clifford. He writes all those faggoty books as Patrick Fitzwilliam."

"OK. Now which one's the victim then, Jack or Fitzwilliam?"

"Maybe the perp read one of his books and, you know... it aroused certain urges. He's obviously a religious fanatic, so being homosexual would be an abomination in his mind."

"He reads one of these books, gets a hard-on, and blames the author."

"He can't fight the urges, so while getting his knob polished, he kills these others as substitutes until he can get to the author, the writer he blames for making him queer."

"What now? He got his target. Now he stops?"

"No." Kasey shook his head and stilled the ball between his hands. "That Leviticus message. He's on a crusade now. Plus he's got a taste for it." He twirled the ball then flipped it off his fingers over to his partner. "He's escalating. I bet he's going to fuck up any little boy-toy that gives him a tickle in his shorts."

Reynaud's phone rang, and he tossed the ball to Kasey before answering. "Reynaud... Yeah, whatcha got?" He grabbed a pen to scribble a few notes. "Yeah, got it. Thanks." He hung up and turned back to Kasey. "They found a match. Our perp's fingerprint matched one from the robbery in Brooklyn."

"You're shitting me. Did they get an ID?"

"Yeah. You aren't going to fucking believe it."

After Taylor drove away from the cabin, Gillian stepped out onto the deck then down to the water, folding her arms around her and rubbing them through her sweater. She peered across the lake to the brilliant colors of the trees, reflected in the sheen of the water. The sun cast a light on the leaves, glistening stacks of gold, silver, and copper coins, as if the trees had been touched by Midas. Her breath visible in the air confirmed Taylor's prediction that soon they would turn brown, wither and blow away, that inevitability of their future a tarnish on their present beauty. She turned away and walked around, gathering sticks and wood for her campfire.

With the pall of Jack's death an ever-present intruder despite Gillian's change in cabins, the evening presented a mosaic of tears, laughter, and moments of contemplative silence; but Taylor touched her. Often. A kiss on the forehead, a hand down her hair. Bringing her wrist to his lips or pulling her into his arms. After dinner and dishes were done, they snuggled on the sofa, her hand in his, drinking wine and basking in the warmth and light from the fireplace.

He pressed his lips against her temple then asked in a teasing tone, "Are you sure you really were a Girl Scout?"

"What're you talking about? Hot dogs are supposed to catch on fire."

"Not in Boy Scouts."

"Just look at this wine." Gillian reached for the bottle on the coffee table in front of them and held the back label for her perusal. "A perfect accompaniment for roasted meat."

"First of all, that was not roasted—that was blackened; and secondly, I wouldn't exactly call that meat."

She leaned on him and giggled against his arm. "I admit, your method was better."

"What's the point of having a cabin with a fireplace

if you aren't going to use it?"

"Well, I do think I did a good job with my campfire."

"Sure. Except for the fact that there's a ban on campfires. I should arrest you."

She slid an arm around his waist. "Does that mean you'd have to frisk me?"

He met her eyes, flames glittering in them, and gave her a quick kiss on the lips. "Not tonight. I have something else in mind."

"Oooh, well, that sounds promising."

"But I don't know. It's really not appropriate for a Girl Scout."

"Hey, not only was I a Girl Scout; I was a Girl Scout Leader."

"You're joking."

"Nope. When my girls were younger, I was the leader of their troop."

He brushed back a few stray hairs that had fallen on her face and spoke in a gravelly voice. "How do you think those parents would feel if they knew their impressionable daughters were in the hands of someone who writes erotica?"

"It's not erotica," she said, her voice low as her eyes darted from his lips then back to his eyes. "It's erotic romance."

"Semantics." He lowered his head, covering her mouth with his as she opened for him, their tongues now in a familiar tango.

He sat back with a smirk. "Are you ready to see what I have planned for you?"

"Definitely."

He stood and held his hand out to help her up. "One thing I like about your new cabin, the bed has a headboard I can tie you to." She didn't budge as he tried to tug her along, and when he looked back, she caught his eyes. "Are you OK with that?"

"Can I ask you something?"

"Anything, sweetheart."

Pink tingeing her cheeks, she blinked with a quick shrug. "Do you…have you done this a lot? Did you and your wife—"

"Never. Like I said with the handcuffs. Not ever until you."

"Why me? Why now?"

He sighed and glanced away for a moment. "Once, a long time ago, I did ask my wife about using handcuffs, but she didn't respond kindly to the idea. Frankly, she was appalled. Now I know, though."

"Know what?"

"About you. You tell me. Do you have experience with this? Did you have a lot of bondage in your past?"

"No, never."

"But it came out in your book. Unlike my ex, you want—no, you need it. When I read your writing, it awoke something inside of me. It just helped me to realize what I need, too."

"And tonight? What do you need?"

He grazed his knuckles down her cheek. "I want to take care of you, help you let everything else that's happening in that brilliant brain of yours drift away, and just be. That's what you need, isn't it? To put your mind to rest and be present now, in the moment?"

"What do you want me to do?"

With a sly grin, he pulled her against him with one arm and raked the other hand up the nape of her neck into her hair, grabbing it into his fist, forcing her head back to accept his kiss. When they parted yet remained still close enough to feed each other's breaths, he stroked his fingers down and around her neck then between her breasts.

"I have something."

Taylor led her to the small table in the entryway where he'd left a shopping bag when he had arrived. From it, he withdrew a full black nylon slip of such cheap quality, it couldn't have cost more than ten dollars.

"I want you to wear this," he said, handing it to her.

"Uh, thank you?"

"It's not a gift, Gillian. Go put it on then meet me in the bedroom."

When she stepped into the bedroom wearing the slip, its lace hem reaching a few inches above the knee, and rubbing her arms for warmth, he had turned down the covers of the bed and taken off his shirt, revealing his broad, muscular chest. His eyes and his smile widened when he saw her.

"That is very sexy."

"Um, all right, but it is also very cold."

"I'll turn the heat up in a moment, but first come over here and sit on the bed."

Following his order, she walked toward him and sat on the edge of the bed facing him. He reached for a long black silk scarf, leaving two other identical scarves lying on the bed. She gaped up at him as he ran the material between his hands.

"How do you feel about being blindfolded? Do you trust me?"

With her eyes downturned, she licked her lips then pulled the lower one into her mouth. When she returned her gaze to his, she nodded. Neither spoke as he wrapped the scarf around her eyes and tied it, their breathing audible in the silence of the room.

As she sat there, plummeted into blackness, she started when he touched her wrist but then relaxed her hand into his. The cool silky fabric skimmed across her arm as he tied a scarf around her wrist. "Too tight?" She swallowed and shook her head. He tied the third scarf around her other wrist in the same manner. "I would have gotten two more scarves, but the sales lady was already giving me funny looks."

"Why two more?"

"For your ankles." Although she couldn't see him, her head jerked in the direction of his voice. "Next time. Now let me help you lie back." He lifted her as he climbed onto the bed, her arms around his neck until he positioned her vertically in the middle of the bed with her head on a pillow. Stretching one arm up, he tied its scarf to the headboard then crawled over her to repeat the process with her other wrist.

Her hardened nipples protruded through the thin black slip. Kneeling over her, he ran his hands down from her bound wrists along her arms then across her breasts, which rose and fell with her accelerating respiration. He massaged them, rubbing the peaks with his thumbs as she lay in total darkness.

"You look good enough to eat." Hunger curved

around every raspy syllable. He scooted back and spread her legs enough for him to reach his hand up to her creamy slit then leaned onto the bed, whispering in her ear. "Oh, yes. You're as turned on as I am. My cock feels like it's going to burst. Too bad you can't feel it, but you will soon enough." As he continued stroking her, he startled her at first when he covered her mouth with a voracious kiss, but she recovered in a split second and matched his fervor. "If I keep this up, I'm going to forget all my plans and just fuck you right now."

"Oh, yes, please."

He chuckled as he pulled his hand out from under her slip then sucked his fingers with a slurp to leave no room for misinterpretation. "I've been patient; you'll have to be, too. I promise it'll be worth the wait. We've had your fantasy, now I get mine." The bed shifted as he stood, then he tossed the covers over her. "I'll be back in a minute."

"You're leaving me like this?"

His fading voice resounded from the doorway. "I'll be right back." Leaving her alone, bound and in darkness, with only her thoughts and the sound of her erratic, shallow breaths.

The wood floor creaked under his bare feet padding across the bedroom, followed by the rivets of his zipper as he pulled off his jeans and tossed them aside. "I told you I'd be right back."

"Where did you go?"

"For one thing," he said, yanking the covers off of her, "to turn the heat up just a tad for you, but I also had to get something."

The springs of the bed squeaked as he joined her there, kneeling above her with his legs on either side of her hips. He bent over and kissed her, her mouth eager to consume his. He grabbed her breasts, pushing them together and rolling her nipples between his thumbs and forefingers. He broke the kiss, his lips trailing down her outstretched neck and along her collar before taking one nipple into his mouth and sucking it through the thin fabric of the black slip as his fingers pulled and pinched the other. Then he reversed the action, suckling the right nipple hard, teasing it with his teeth, while tugging on the stiff, damp peak of the other breast. She lay back, releasing low guttural noises and gripping the scarves holding her in bondage.

He shifted off of her then, moving back beside her legs and lifting the hem of the slip directly between her thighs. Kneeling over her, he said, "God, you are so tempting, but I think you are sexier without lingerie."

The cold steel blade touched her flesh, the shock of it causing her sudden, sharp intake of breath, with the sound of tearing fabric ricocheting off the walls.

"Wh-what is that?"

"What does it feel like?"

"Cold metal. Is that a knife?"

"Shhh…"

As he worked his way up, cutting the slip through the center, he allowed his finger one stroke up the lips at the juncture of her thighs, and she hissed.

"Sorry, I couldn't resist." His voice low and rough.

He sliced through the thin material splitting the slip

in two, each *clip-clip-clip* revealing more of her until she lay bare. The cool air of the room wafted over her skin, teasing her nipples and stealing her breath.

No light shone from beneath the closed door to the silent room.

She hesitated, her hand trembling as she turned the doorknob, although she knew the room would be empty.

He shouldn't even be in town.

He definitely shouldn't be in his office, but neither should she. Something drove her to go in there, either jealousy or a suspicion of something more.

How idiotic she had sounded on the phone when his colleague had called. "I thought he was with you," she'd said. From the pause and then the tone of his voice on the other end of the line, his friend's thoughts had followed the same path as her own. To another woman.

Flummoxed by his faux pas—the unwritten, or sometimes written, rule that men would cover for the indiscretions of other members of their sex—he stuttered and tripped over his words.

"He probably just got caught up in all that traffic."

"His cell is rolling straight to voicemail."

"Um, the battery must be dead." But his tone was too earnest not to know that he *would never leave without a car charger.*

No, he *was not the type to leave things to chance. If anyone could get away with cheating, he could.*

She stared at his desk, clean, neat, everything perfectly in place. No computer. He would have taken his laptop with him. "Out of town." She walked around and sat in his chair and began opening the drawers, searching for some clue but coming up empty. He had a file cabinet, but she found it full of old files and nothing else. Likewise, a thorough search of the bookshelves turned up nothing but books.

Sitting in his chair, she tapped her fingers on its arms, her eyes roaming around the walls as thoughts rolled around in her head. No, he would never leave evidence of an affair here where she had access, nowhere that she could potentially find it.

Then she spotted it—a plastic storage bin on top of the bookshelf. Even he would not be so meticulous as to organize his indiscretions, would he? But the longer she stared at it, the more she had to know what it contained. Even standing on a chair she couldn't reach it. She walked out of his office then returned with a broom, which she used to nudge the container to the edge of the bookcase, exerting more effort than she would've thought necessary. What could he have in there that was so heavy?

Because of its weight, she had to take care not to lose her footing, skidding it down the bookcase then balancing it on the back of the chair as she stepped down. She set it down on the floor and knelt beside it, her hands shaking as she tried to open it, but it had to be just from the exertion of bringing it down. What could he possibly have hidden in such a common, benign storage bin?

She cracked open the lid, but what she found inside

confused her, drawing her brows together. She removed the items one by one, carefully so she could replace them exactly as he had had them. First one Bible, then another, and a third—all well-worn with dog-eared pages. Throughout each of them, passages had been underlined with a firm but shaky hand; and from one of the Bibles, several pages were ripped or torn out. Setting those aside, she next found loose pages from a novel. Pricked by Thorns. *Her fingers trembled and her pulse raced as she scanned the pages, many with brown stains, and each one a scene of explicit sex.*

Tears filled her eyes as she pulled out the iPad and laptop and turned them both on. Next, a man's thin wallet and a smartphone. She wiped her eyes with her hands, glanced up at the ceiling, and took a deep breath before opening the wallet. The driver's license of Jack Clifford, credit cards with the same name, even cash. Four twenty-dollar bills, marred with bloody fingerprints.

She wept as she reached for the final item in the bin: a small rectangular box in a Ziploc bag. She pulled out the white cardboard box, one that might have contained a newly-purchased necklace. With her heart throbbing in her throat but with no notion of what she would find, she lifted the lid.

She screamed as she dropped it and backed away, pushing herself across the floor until her back was against the wall. She sat there in horror as her mixture of shrieking and sobbing continued. The approaching sirens echoed her screams, as if the police had learned the truth a split-second after she did, like a dash indicator warning of slick ice with the car already spinning out of control.

The darkness behind the blindfold heightened all other sensual perception: His weight on the bed, his hands on her breasts, the sound of her own panting as his tongue blazed a path down her torso to the heat between her legs. The quiet of the room amplified her soft moans as he licked up and down her cleft then dove his tongue into her core. He stopped only long enough to rasp out, "God, you taste good. I cannot wait to fuck you," then returned to his task.

She twisted her thumbs around her restraints, tightening them as the firm tip of his tongue rolled around her clit, teasing and taunting as she squirmed on the bed, alternating between holding her breath and gasping for air. Then he drove his fingers inside of her, pushing up as his tongue lapped down. With rhythmic precision, his fingers probed within her in time with his tongue's violent attention. The vivid sensations forced her to cry out as wave after wave of ecstasy rolled over her.

The Lord God's servant watched her.

The Sword of Michael the Archangel bore witness to how this Jezebel has no shame in her nudity, as Eve in the Garden before the Fall. Like Bathsheba before her, she tempts men into adultery with her bare flesh.

As with the demon Lilith, she shuns subservience but instead perverts and entices men to serve her with sapphistry. This self-styled prophetess lies naked in the manner of Saul and the true prophets while leading this man into sexual immorality, writhing beneath his mouth.

I will cast her on a bed of suffering, and all of those who have known the depths of Satan and commit adultery with her will suffer intensely, and I will strike her children dead.

The Sword's power and wrath grew harder as he watched the Jezebel with this man, another servant of the Lord she has led astray. He mounted her mouth, and she pleasured him in the manner of the Sodomites, the lines of the muscles of his back and buttocks with beauty to rival Absalom, but Absalom was not a righteous man. He did not see his own sinfulness and thus the Lord God found it right that he be speared in the heart.

The Sword of Michael witnessed Jezebel's whoredoms as she seduces the Lord's servant to lie with her, as he pushes her knees back, his firm thighs and buttocks flexing with each thrust inside of her as she thrashes against him. Just as she leads him into immorality and adultery, with her sorcery she has forced the Sword to spill his seed on the ground like the sinner Onan.

Now the works of the flesh are manifest: adultery, fornication, uncleanness, lasciviousness. The Sword has given them time to repent their immorality, but they are unwilling. The adulterer and the adulteress shall surely be put to death.

Chapter 13

Taylor released Gillian from her silk bondage while she drifted in the oxytocin afterglow of her orgasms. Once untied, each arm flopped lifeless onto the bed as her breathing and pulse slowly returned to normal. He slid the scarf over her forehead, their eyes meeting for the first time since she had first sat down on the bed, and they smiled and gazed at each other. Even in the coolness of the room, a sheen of sweat glistened on their skin.

"Hi," he said, his hand brushing over the top of her head.

"Hi."

"That was…"

"Intense," she said.

"Yes. Intense." He brought his lips to hers, so sweet and gentle, in complete contrast to their fevered, rabid lovemaking. "Are you all right?"

"Oh, yes. Even better."

He pulled the sheet over them and rolled back against the bed, cradling her against him. "Good."

"And this was your fantasy?"

"I have been wanting to rip those dresses off of you

since the first time I saw you in one when we danced at Oktoberfest. I decided a cheap slip might be a better idea."

"Uh, yeah. You're not tearing up my clothes."

"Then I thought ripping it off would be too quick." He picked up the scissors and showed them to her. "I decided to cut it off slowly, inch by inch, building the anticipation."

"Whew. Can we do it again?"

He muffled his chuckling in her hair against her neck. "After this week? I might need a few days to recuperate."

"A few *days!*"

"Hey, I'm not nineteen, you know. You at least have to give me until morning."

"Maybe I should find me a nineteen-year-old."

He pulled her tighter against him and kissed her forehead. "They couldn't handle you."

With her fingers fondling his chest hair, she sighed. "I know. And I wouldn't want one."

They both stared off in opposite directions, keeping their thoughts to themselves. Eventually, she said, "What do you want to do now?"

He kissed her eyebrow. "I want to marry you."

"Oh, come on." She grinned and shoved him in the ribs.

"I mean it. Marry me, Gillian."

"The ink isn't even dry on my divorce decree. You're talking out of your orgasm."

"You know it's more than that. I can't do *casual* with you. I told you I'm in love with you. Sooner or later, you'll admit it, too. I've fallen hard and fast because nothing has ever felt so right, so…natural." He intertwined his fingers with hers upon his chest. "We're a perfect fit. Sweetheart, I'm a very possessive man, and I want the world to know you belong to me."

"What? Do you want me to wear a collar around my neck, too?"

"Maybe, but for now I'll be satisfied with a ring on your finger."

She squeezed her eyes closed tight, her brows drawn together, and her lips disappeared into her mouth, tension wrapping around her face for several moments as she held her breath. When she finally relaxed and released it, she let the topic go as well. "Actually, when I asked what you wanted to do *now*, I meant in the immediate future—like right now. Do you want to go to sleep? Are you hungry? Do you want to…well, there's no TV. Read?"

"You know, I am a little hungry."

"I still have that can of tamales."

"You know what I was thinking? We could probably get that fire going again. You up for a s'more?"

She tilted her head back and looked up at him with smiling eyes. "I thought you said I had to wait until tomorrow."

"For that, yes, but I have read that chocolate has the same chemical reaction in the brain as sex."

"I think you read too much."

He grinned and kissed the tip of her nose. "You feel like roasting marshmallows?"

"Of course! I'm a Girl Scout."

He slipped away from her and stood, walking naked

across the room to pull on his jeans. "The ingredients are still at my cabin. Why don't you stoke the fire, and I'll be right back with the graham crackers and marshmallows."

Once dressed, Taylor jumped in his police cruiser to drive the short distance up to his own cabin, but halfway there, his steering wheel began to shake, followed by the unmistakable clunking of his rear wheel, the flat tire forcing him to pull off the road and onto the driveway of an abandoned cabin. He hopped out of the car just long enough to confirm his suspicion then jumped back in and grabbed the two-way.

"Gillian. Over." He waited a few moments then repeated, "Gillian. Over."

Her voice rose through the static. "Uh, yes, I'm here. Over."

"Just wanted to let you know I'll be a few more minutes. I got a flat—must have picked up a nail somewhere—but I'm going to wait and change it in the morning. So I'll hoof it over there and be back as soon as I can. Over."

"Uh...OK. Oh. Over."

He zipped up his jacket. "Is everything all right? Over."

"Yeah. It's, uh, that'll give me more time to get this fire going. It doesn't want to cooperate. Over."

His shoulders rose with his suppressed chuckle. "OK, Miss Girl Scout, just don't put kerosene on it. Over."

"Damn. That was going to be my next move. Over."

"See you in a few. Over and out."

"Over and out."

Taylor dug out a spare flashlight then got out and slammed the car door. He cut across the neighboring cabins' property down to the lake path and walked on to his cabin. When he got to his door, he found an envelope wedged against the jamb above the knob. He closed the door behind him and stepped over to the lamp table to open the envelope. His blood turned to ice as he read the handwritten words on the sheet of paper:

Thou sufferest the woman Jezebel, who calleth herself a prophetess; and she teacheth and seduceth my servants to commit fornication. I gave her time that she should repent; and she willeth not to repent of her fornication. Behold, I cast her into bed, and them that commit adultery with her into great tribulation, and I will kill her children with death; and all the churches shall know that I am he that searcheth the reins and hearts.

And of Jezebel also spoke the Lord, saying, the dogs shall eat Jezebel. Her body will be eaten by dogs and there won't be enough left of her to bury. This is the Word of the Lord our God.

Taylor pressed the talk button on the two-way and shouted, "Gillian! Gillian! They're here! Go—"

Gillian knelt on the floor in front of the fireplace, rearranging the wood on the grate and banging the glowing embers, lighting twisted pieces of newspaper and sticking them under the log but failing in her efforts to ignite a flame.

Static from the radio beside her caught her attention, then Sam yelling.

"Gillian! Gillian! They're here! Go—" Then nothing.

She stared at the two-way, waiting, with a frown. He hadn't said "Over," and she hesitated before picking it up and pressing the talk button. "Sam? Over."

The radio emitted an eerie silence.

She stood and tossed the fire poker aside then tried again. "Sam? Are you there? Over."

He hadn't said what was where. He hadn't said where she should go. She slipped on her shoes and pulled a sweater over her dress, then she grabbed her coat and her car keys, along with the two-way, and ran out to her car.

At the moment she discovered her flat tires, a menacing voice bled out of the radio. "Gillian…" A male voice, somehow familiar but distorted, a man possessed, obsessed. "I hope you enjoyed your final fuck. Your friend is lying here with a knife in his back."

The blood drained from Gillian's face, leaving her light-headed as her heart raced out of control. Her entire body quivered, causing her to drop the keys as she held tight to the two-way. "Gillian, I know you can hear me. I watched you with him through the window. I saw how you seduced him into perversions. Come here and see the destruction you have wrought, witness the wrath of God, who condemns all sodomites and adulterers to death."

She dropped her coat and covered her mouth with her hand as tears prickled behind her eyes. "No...no..." she repeated, shaking her head.

"You did this, Gillian. You brought death upon him by seducing him into fornication."

"The radio," she whispered on one of her clouds of breath. She ran up the drive to the road, rushing toward Taylor's abandoned police car.

The demonic voice taunted her. "You drove that knife so deep into his back, I couldn't even get it out. That's OK. He had plenty of knives there to arm the Sword of Michael the Archangel for this mission."

The word "there" brought her to a halt. If the killer wasn't *there* at Taylor's cabin, he was somewhere with her in the dark. He would be looking for her, hunting her, listening for her. She glanced at the two-way in her hand then hurled it as far in the opposite direction as she could and ran away. She spotted the cruiser in the distance just off the road, and she stayed hidden behind each cabin that stood between her and the car, checking behind her and around each corner as she approached the vehicle.

Finally she reached it and jumped inside. She closed and locked the door then grabbed the mic off the police radio and held it to her mouth. "Hello, hello. Can anyone hear me?" She pulled the mic and discovered that the coiled cable had been cut at the same time the cold air coming through the broken passenger-side window struck her face.

Then she glimpsed a shadow in the rearview mirror. A man dressed all in black marched with purpose toward the squad car. He wore a hoodie with a jacket over it, and an old fashioned knit ski mask covered his face. He held the two-way in one hand and a flashlight in the other, but somewhere he had a knife on him as well.

Gillian jumped out of the car and ran down to the lake side of the next cabin. She ran up to the door but found it locked. She crouched down close to the ground and against the house, watching for him. He had last been on the road, but he must have seen her run down toward the lake. She covered her mouth with her icy hand and listened for any sound other than the chorus of insects, frogs, and owls—ominous in their difference from the sounds of the city. She heard a woman's scream from across the lake, but Taylor had told her it was a fox the first night he walked her home. Tears streamed down and over the hand she still held against her mouth.

The crunch of twigs and shuffle of leaves followed her trail—*he* had followed her trail. Only two more cabins lay between her and Taylor's. Staying low and with her back against the wall, she edged over to the far corner and peeked around it. She slid along the side wall back up toward the road, constantly checking behind her and watching her step to avoid twigs or anything else that would reveal her location.

Then she heard that voice sing out her name. "Gillian…" It reverberated through the two-way she had tossed away, but both came from down near her cabin. "You know you cannot run from your fate. This is the will of God." He had to be down by the lake, walking away from her.

She ran up the road as fast as she could until she reached Taylor's cabin, then she scurried down to the porch facing the lake and inside, slamming and locking the door. She turned around, and her blood-curdling shriek could never be confused with a fox. Taylor lay prone on the floor, not moving, his face turned away, and a knife jammed into the back of his neck.

"No! No! No!" she screamed and wept as she fell to her knees beside him. She lifted his hand, still warm against her freezing fingers and damp cheeks as she kissed the back of it and held it against her face.

The pounding of boots on the porch jerked her around, and she dropped his hand and stood up. *He* jiggled the doorknob before landing a kick against the wood. After a quick scan of the room, Gillian dashed into Taylor's bedroom and locked the door. His gun lay on the dresser in its holster, and she reached it as the front door splintered open. She took hold of it with trembling fingers, checked the safety, then leaned against the far wall gripping the gun between her shaking hands, aimed at the door.

She cried out each time he kicked the bedroom door until he burst in, knife in hand. The tears in her eyes did not affect her aim as she fired into his chest, once, twice, again and again, his body recoiling with each bullet until he fell backwards onto the floor.

Sobbing in near hysterics, she slid her back down the wall and sat with the gun in one hand upon her bent knees, pointed toward the doorway, her other hand covering her eyes. A thud brought her hands back around the gun, trained on the man in black, but he remained quite dead. The heavy footfall in the next room had her scrambling to her feet. She wiped her arm across her eyes, drying her tears, and took a deep, staggering breath. She stood ready for anything that came through that doorway.

Except this.

She screamed as Taylor stumbled in, his hand on the back of his head, the brows over his dazed eyes vacillating between wrinkling together and rising up his forehead. Undeterred by her screaming, his gaze dropped to the dead man on his bedroom floor as he took another step in.

Gillian's screams morphed into sobbing cries and whispered "No"s as her head shook slowly back and forth. Taylor lifted his eyes to her, blinking several times to bring her into focus.

"Gillian, my god. Thank god you're OK." He dropped his hand from his head and moved toward her but stopped when she held the gun pointed at his heart.

"St-Stop!"

"What…What is it?"

"You're one of them. You're with the Sword of Saint Michael."

"What the hell are you talking about?"

"You…and he…" She tilted the nose of the gun toward the body for a split second. "You're with him!"

"Come on, Gillian. Do you really think I would fuck you like I did tonight if I were some deranged religious zealot? OK, wait. Don't answer that. Just tell me he didn't hurt you."

"I saw you! He stabbed you! I saw the knife in your back! What was it? A trick knife? Some sort of prop?"

"No, he didn't. He clubbed me over the head from behind when I was trying to reach you on the radio—to warn you."

"He said he killed you! I saw the knife myself!"

"Sweetheart, no, he didn't stab me. I don't have a knife in my back." He turned around, the handle of a knife protruding from his neck with blood streaming down his back, setting her shrieking again.

"It…it's still there!"

With his neck twisted as far as it would go, he turned in circles like a dog chasing its own tail until she laughed and cried simultaneously. He faced her and stopped turning then lifted his hand to the back of his neck, and he touched the knife.

"Holy fuck!" With his eyes as wide as saucers, he grabbed hold of the handle.

"No! Don't pull it out! Leave it or you could bleed out or maybe cause more damage."

"Like having a knife jammed into my neck isn't enough!"

"It…it doesn't hurt?"

"Well, it didn't until you told me about it! Please, can I please just hold you? Keep the gun on me if you don't trust me, but, Christ, I just want to know you're all right."

"No." She placed the gun on the dresser and ran to him. "I do trust you. Implicitly."

He squeezed her as tightly as his shocked muscles would allow. "Did he hurt you? Did he cut you?" She shook her head against his chest. "Were there…were there any dogs?"

Wrapped in each other's arms, she raised her face to him with a crease between her brows. "What?"

The distant wail of approaching sirens whistled on the wind outside.

"I thought…Jesus, I thought…"

Although she smiled, the silent tears still flowed. "I thought you were dead. I mean, I *knew* you were dead. I don't care if it's been five days, five hours, five weeks, or five years. I love you, Samuel Taylor. I do."

"I wish I didn't have to *die* for you to admit it, but I'll take it." He kissed the top of her head and rested his cheek upon it. "You know I love you. I don't want to live without you."

She squeezed her eyes shut and her arms around him. "I know. Me, either. But right now, I think you should sit down until we can get an ambulance." She stepped back to help him sit on the bed.

"To tell you the truth, I am feeling a little lightheaded. I think I should lie down."

"No!" She held him about the waist with a quick glimpse at the knife jutting out of his neck. "I don't think lying down is a good idea."

He rubbed the knot on his head and dropped his gaze to the masked man dead not far from his feet. "So who is this fuck?"

As the sirens grew louder, she asked, "Shouldn't we wait until the police get here?"

"I am the fucking police! Unmask the bastard."

She stepped over and kicked the knife away then knelt beside the body and peeled up the mask. She squealed and fell back against the bed frame, the man's dead eyes staring at the ceiling.

"Do you know him?"

"It's…it's Jacob, Sarah's husband. My agent's husband."

Chapter 14

"He's extraordinarily lucky, Ms. Tate," the doctor at the NYU hospital said two days after Taylor's surgery. "A fraction of an inch either way, the knife would have hit his spinal cord or an artery."

As soon as the police had arrived at the scene, they had radioed and had Taylor medevac'd to New York City while they forced Gillian to remain behind for questioning.

"So he's going to be OK?" Gillian asked, standing beside Taylor's hospital bed with her hand on his shoulder.

"The knife was lodged in bone, so it did damage his neck. Fortunately, nothing life-threatening or any possibility of paralysis."

"And so he can really be released today?"

"As long as he takes it easy and has the wound checked regularly for the next few weeks. I wouldn't suggest any long drives for a while either."

She smiled at Taylor. "This will be a role reversal. I get to take care of you for a change. How would you like to be pampered in a New York penthouse for a while?"

"As long as you're there, I think I'd go anywhere to get out of here," Taylor said, "although I will miss the morphine."

"As soon as they finish up the paperwork, you're good to go," the doctor said. "I'm sorry about the job, Mr. Taylor, but, uh." He glanced up at Gillian then back to Taylor. "Congratulations."

When the doctor had gone, Gillian turned to Taylor. "What did he mean by that?"

"The job? Well, because of the neck injury, my career in law enforcement has come to an end."

Her hand flew to her face, muffling her gasp. "Oh, no! Sam, I am so, so sorry."

He took her hand and, meeting her eyes, brought it to his lips. "I'm not. Hell, I could be dead or paralyzed. Now I just have early retirement. Even though I wasn't officially 'on the job,' they're still considering it an injury in the line of duty since I was protecting a citizen, although I did a piss-poor job of it."

"What are you talking about? If it weren't for me, you never would have been hurt, and—"

"Now, sweetheart, you are going to have to stop blaming yourself for the actions of some deranged religious zealot!"

"*And*...if it weren't for you, I'd be dead right now."

"How do you figure that?"

"You insisted on the two-way radios, you called to warn me he was there, and you just happened to have a gun." She looked down but as if viewing something far in the distance. "I still can't believe I killed someone...and someone I knew."

"You had no choice. Nothing could have stopped him. He would have killed you. He wasn't the man you thought you knew. Hey, you brought me some clothes, right? Help me get out of this dress."

She helped him sit up, and he pulled his legs around as she got the bag with his belongings. "Sarah's gone. Moved in with her mother and won't take my calls. She'll never forgive me."

"Or maybe she won't forgive herself." Taylor pulled on his jeans as Gillian untied the back of his hospital gown. "Her husband not only tried to kill you but killed your best friend."

"Jack's dead. Sarah's gone. They were my only friends."

"You have me."

After a tap on the door, a nurse poked her head in. "Chief Taylor, there are a couple of detectives here to see you and Miss Tate."

The two men walked in as Taylor finished buttoning his shirt with Gillian sitting on the bed. "I'm Detective Kasey; this is Detective Reynaud."

He shook their hands in turn. "Sam Taylor. Have you met Ms. Tate?"

"No, good to finally meet you."

Gillian stood and stepped toward the men. "So what did you find out about the Sword of Michael the Archangel?"

"As far as we have been able to determine," Reynaud said, "Jacob Falgert *was* the Sword of Michael."

"I don't understand. Who broke into their house?"

"He 'broke in' to his own house," Kasey said. "He

left his men's Bible study or whatever without his wife's knowledge so he could steal her laptop and try to find out where you'd gone. Then he went back to the church and came home with her to report it. We matched the print from the Clifford crime scene to the elimination print they had taken when investigating the robbery."

"And is that why he killed Jack? To try to find me?"

"It appears so. He had become obsessed with you."

She frowned and shook her head. "Why? I don't understand."

"From what we've found on his computer—" Reynaud said, "quite the manifesto—at first he resented you for his wife's success, her sudden independence, and after your divorce, he thought his marriage was in trouble, too."

"Then he read the manuscript for your second book," said Kasey, "and it seemed to have aroused these homosexual urges he had been trying to suppress for decades."

"Oh, my god." She covered her face with her hands, and Taylor folded his arms around her. "I cannot believe I set this off with words—with what I wrote."

"Shhh…" Taylor said. "You can't blame yourself for writing a good book. Something would have set him off eventually."

"What about the two other men?"

Kasey said, "Random pick-ups. We're now looking into similar unsolved cases from over the last twenty-five years. Taylor's right, Ms. Tate. You are not responsible for his actions. From the delusions evident in his writings, his mental state had been deteriorating for some time. He had never been stable. We've already linked him to another homicide when he was in college."

She turned back to the detectives with glassy eyes. "But I am to blame for his victims. Poor Jack. Plus he almost killed Sam. And Sarah had no idea?"

"She says no, not until he kept changing his plans about going to Boston, evidently based on where he thought you were going to be, but then his law partner called looking for him. That's when his wife got suspicious and found the, uh, evidence in his home office—her laptop, Mr. Clifford's cell phone, Bibles— but by then we'd made a positive ID on the fingerprint."

The detectives gave them their cards and made their final goodbyes as Taylor sat down and pulled on his shoes.

Once alone, she said, "I just still am in shock that my novel did this."

He stood and grasped her arms, forcing her to look at him. "Gillian, he just used that as an excuse. How many millions of people have read your books without going on murderous rampages? From his rantings, clearly he was in the middle of a psychotic break. As for the gay sex, he wouldn't have been able to suppress his urges forever. You were just someone convenient for him to blame, and he picked through the Bible and took lines out of context to support his delusions."

"But even you said my writing inspired certain

urges for you."

"You see? More evidence of the positive effect of your writing." He smiled and kissed her lips. "The pen really is mightier than the Sword."

"*Ugh*." He laughed as she dropped her head against his chest. "How long have you been waiting to use that line?"

He kissed the top of her head. "Only the last day or so." He stepped back and closed up his bag. "Now when can I get out of here?"

"I hope you don't mind. I did have to go inside your house in town to get you more clothes since you mainly had uniforms in the cabin."

"Did you check on the girl in the pit?"

"She's fine," she said as they headed out. "I gave her a poodle to keep her company."

"That's good. Now let's go check out your BDSM dungeon."

"Man, are you going to be disappointed." Then she stopped and turned back to him. "Hey, there was something else the doctor said. Why did he say, 'Congratulations'?"

"Oh, yeah. Well." He turned back to her with his brows raised and a smile twitching on his mouth. "Remember, I was kind of doped up, but when he said I had to quit the police, I said now you wouldn't have a reason not to marry me."

"Marry you?"

His grin broadened, and he glanced down at his shoes then back at her. "Yeah."

"You're still on that?"

"Well, if I'm going to be staying in your penthouse,

what kind of example would you be setting for the Girl Scouts of the world if you were living in sin?"

"And what about when I'm traveling all over the world doing promotions?"

"I figured I'd go with you, maybe be like your manager-slash-bodyguard."

The corners of her lips lifted as her eyes widened. "Oh, you did, did you?"

He pulled her toward him, his mouth hovering over hers. "You know I like taking care of you, and I think you need it."

"But I said I'd never get married again."

"You also told me all of your stories have to end with a happily ever after. This is your story," he said just before his lips met hers.

The end.

If you enjoyed *DEADLINE*, you will love:

Alicia's Possession
by Colette L. Saucier

"Murder, Mystery, love, BDSM, and some great sex. When I read a book and I can feel the characters emotions, then I know it's a good book." —Between the Sheets Book Reviews

Haunted by a traumatic accident and her husband's betrayal, Alicia believes she can never trust again. Now she must surrender her will to Mason if she wants to find out if the bizarre events terrorizing her are the work of the paranormal, her own paranoia, or something far more sinister.

After recovering from a freak car crash that put her in a coma and left her with no memory of the accident, wealthy socialite Alicia Pageant becomes convinced there is a connection between the mysterious disappearance of her neighbor and a series of bizarre occurrences inside her own house; but everyone—including the detective called to investigate—thinks the woman's head injury has left her unable to distinguish reality from fantasy.

As Detective Mason Crawley investigates this "suspicious incident," Alicia's palpable sadness and vulnerability awaken his instinct to protect her and lead her into the light; but when her story begins to unravel, each new piece of information creates more questions than it answers. He begins to wonder if he is falling in love with a woman who is a witness to a cleverly-concealed crime, dangerously delusional, or a murderer.

"A good read for both the love story and the mystery."
— Manic Readers

Also by Scarlet Hawthorne

Between the Notes

"Sweet & funny! A wonderful story of finding courage through love to come out and be yourself."

When an underage groupie stows away on his tour bus to be near her idol, rock superstar Damon Frost suddenly finds himself facing serious charges and a federal prosecutor out for blood. He could easily prove his innocence but only by revealing the secret he has hidden in the closet for years, destroying his image as a sex symbol.

Damon thinks a deal offered by US attorney Michael Rellman will save his reputation as a ladies man, but what will protect him from his growing feelings for the handsome prosecutor and the risk to his career?

"There are funny moments and sad moments. The intimate moments in which they talk and learn who they are are beautiful and poignant. They give us insight as to what drives them and what they desire. The other intimate moments are sexy and sweet because we see love and respect shine through. These two men will capture your heart and have you root for them to come together and stay together." —Hello Booklover

About the Author

www.ScarletHawthorne.com
Lover of beauty, wine, and laughter.
Writer of sultry erotic romance.

Occupation: Author
Location: New Orleans
Interests: Red wine, black coffee, dark chocolate, deep kisses
Favorite drink: St~Germain cocktail
Favorite flower: Gardenia
Favorite song: "Maggot Brain" by Funkadelic
Favorite book: *Slaughterhouse-Five* by Kurt Vonnegut
Favorite spice: Cumin
Favorite author: Anaïs Nin
Favorite film: *Secretary*
Favorite quote: "I believe in pink. I believe that laughing is the best calorie burner. I believe in kissing, kissing a lot. I believe in being strong when everything seems to be going wrong. I believe that happy girls are the prettiest girls. I believe that tomorrow is another day, and I believe in miracles." ~Audrey Hepburn